On the spur of the moment, Tyler switched strategies

He curved his hands around her waist and pulled her up.

"Oh!" Remy's hands went to his shoulders. And then, because he couldn't resist, he swung her in a half circle and kissed her cheek when he set her down.

She gripped his shoulders to steady herself. "What was that for?"

"No special reason. I just wanted to say welcome aboard."

Then, before she knew it, he lowered his head and kissed her. Hitting her mouth this time instead of her cheek.

And then before she could analyze that, he kissed her again. This time more softly. Slowly. She couldn't help but respond in kind. Tilting her head a bit, she kissed him back. Stepped a little closer.

Tyler Mann was a guy who knew how to kiss.

Dear Reader,

Thank you for picking up *Second Chance Hero*, my eighth Harlequin American Romance!

Ramona Greer, the heroine of this book, first appeared in *Baby Makes Six*. I had intended to just have her be a very minor character, but the next thing I knew, I was dressing Ramona in beautiful designer suits, giving her a nickname, and making up a whole backstory for her. In short, Ramona stuck with me!

A few months later, we flew to Florida for vacation. When I was I flipping through the in-flight magazine, I saw a picture of an attractive lady with very sad eyes who worked for the airline. As the hours passed, I kept staring at the photo and read her very brief, very succinct biography. While I did, I kept wondering about everything that *wasn't* said. Unlike the other employees' bios, there was no mention of a spouse or children. Nothing was written about her favorite hobbies. And, well, that kind of bothered me.

So, I did what any other writer would do—I made up reasons for that. A few moments later, I knew I had a story, and I knew that "mystery woman" in the magazine was Ramona Greer. So, here's one of my favorite books, ever.

I love to hear from readers. Please visit my Web site and say hello! Or, stop by our Harlequin American Blog, www.harauthors.blogspot.com, and visit me there.

All my best,

Shelley Galloway

www.shelleygalloway.com

Second Chance Hero

SHELLEY GALLOWAY

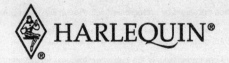

HARLEQUIN®

TORONTO • NEW YORK • LONDON
AMSTERDAM • PARIS • SYDNEY • HAMBURG
STOCKHOLM • ATHENS • TOKYO • MILAN • MADRID
PRAGUE • WARSAW • BUDAPEST • AUCKLAND

Recycling programs
for this product may
not exist in your area.

ISBN-13: 978-0-373-75316-1

SECOND CHANCE HERO

Copyright © 2010 by Shelley Sabga.

This edition published by arrangement with Harlequin Books S.A.

For questions and comments about the quality of this book please contact us at *Customer_eCare@Harlequin.ca*

® and TM are trademarks of the publisher. Trademarks indicated with ® are registered in the United States Patent and Trademark Office, the Canadian Trade Marks Office and in other countries.

www.eHarlequin.com

Printed in U.S.A.

ABOUT THE AUTHOR

Most mornings, Shelley Galloway can be found typing at her computer with a large cup of coffee and two dogs by her side. She loves to write stories for Harlequin American Romance about small towns, large families and people she would like to know.

Shelley also loves to shop, go for walks and talk about her miniature dachshund, Suzy. She does not like to organize anything, lift weights or balance her checkbook. Shelley also writes Amish inspirational romances as Shelley Shepard Gray.

Shelley lives in southern Ohio with her husband and family. She loves to hear from readers and can be found blogging at www.harauthors.blogspot.com, or contacted via her Web site, www.shelleygalloway.com.

Books by Shelley Galloway

HARLEQUIN AMERICAN ROMANCE

1090—CINDERELLA CHRISTMAS
1134—SIMPLE GIFTS
1156—A SMALL-TOWN GIRL
1183—THE GOOD MOTHER
1212—THE MOMMY BRIDE
1244—MOMMY IN TRAINING
1291—BABY MAKES SIX

To my editor, Johanna Raisanen.
Your encouragement and expertise always make me
a better writer. Thank you, and thank you again.

Chapter One

She was nervous.

Why was she nervous? Ramona Greer crossed her legs, shifted and smoothed her skirt. Tapped the end of her pen against the spiral notebook perched on her lap. Reread the résumé in her hand and weighed the pros and cons of the candidate's qualifications.

Oh, who was she kidding? She wasn't thinking about work experience and reference checks. No, she was thinking how Tyler Mann was one of the most charismatic men she'd ever met.

And *that* was making her nervous.

Every few minutes Remy found herself examining the way his raven-black hair curled just-so-right over his left eyebrow. And sitting so close to him, she could see his eyes really were a silky chocolate-brown.

And that dress shirt—it was obviously European. The white fabric had a soft sheen to it, and the shirt had a more tailored fit than the ones most men wore in the office. And—what a fit that was. The fabric glided over his arms and chest, making it impossible not to notice that he definitely enjoyed working out. On a daily basis.

He stared at her directly. "Is there anything else you want to know about me, Ms. Greer?"

Nothing that was any of her business! "No." When his eyebrow rose, she tried again. "I mean to say your résumé is certainly impressive. But I'm afraid I still don't quite understand why you're interested in working at Carnegie, Mr. Mann. With a background in computer software, you could work somewhere else and earn far more money, not to mention be more challenged."

"I imagine answering the phones could be challenging. And doing any job well can create quite a bit of satisfaction, don't you think?"

The question hung there like a piñata hanging from a string, darting back and forth. She searched for a suitable reply. "Yes," she said finally. "I imagine any job could create, um, satisfaction."

"I'm glad we agree on that." He smiled appreciatively. "You know, I've flown all over the country for the past ten years and chased accounts. I've worked more weekends, late nights and holidays than I care to admit. Now I just want a job that I can leave at the end of my shift and forget about." He leaned forward, bracing his elbows on his knees. "I hope you don't find that off-putting."

"No, not at all." What she found off-putting was that his new position gave her yet more interesting angles to look at. Oh, she felt like a dirty old woman.

She straightened, striving to put herself back in professional mode. After all, interviewing call-center representatives for Carnegie Airlines was nothing new. She'd conducted dozens of these in the past four or five years.

Yet—when was the last time she'd shifted so much in her chair that the skirt of her suit edged halfway up her thighs? Fumbling with his résumé, she glanced his way again.

Only to see that his gaze had darted to her nylon-covered legs.

Oh, yes. Tyler Mann had noticed the state of her skirt. As discreetly as possible she tugged the hem down to her knees.

Focusing on work once again, she murmured, "I should warn you that although you might find the hours a breeze, the job certainly is not. People who call us want all kinds of information from Carnegie Airlines. You'll handle everything from customer complaints about flight attendants to panicked people needing an emergency flight. Sometimes the calls and requests can be demanding."

If anything, her comment seemed to amuse him. "I can be demanding, too."

The temperature in the room rose another ten degrees.

Remy stood up, teetering only an instant in her black four- inch heels. "Well, then, there's nothing else to do but offer you a job, Mr. Mann." She held out a hand.

He took it. "Please call me Tyler, Ms. Greer." Curving his palm around hers, he somehow managed to combine the perfect amount of firmness with tenderness, as if he was afraid he'd crush her bones. It was disconcerting.

But, of course, so was that smile. "I'm Ramona. Remy." Why had she said that? Hardly anyone at Carnegie called her anything but Ramona or Ms. Greer.

His gazed warmed. "Remy, it's been a pleasure to meet you."

"Yes." She crossed to her desk and hastily picked up a file folder. "This is your new employee packet. You'll find pretty much everything self-explanatory. I won't bore you by going through the employee handbook and insurance information just now. The folks in human resources will walk you through it all. Finally, don't forget to stop at Shawn Wagner's desk on the way out. She'll be in charge of your training."

"I'll do that." But to her surprise, he didn't move. Instead, he looked at her directly. "So, will I see you again?"

"Excuse me?"

"I just wondered if you were the type of woman who stayed up here in your office, or if you roamed the cubicle aisles."

"I roam." Remy looked away. Hoped that he didn't spy her looking completely flustered. Because, well, she was.

After a significant pause, he stepped back. "Well, then, I'll look forward to seeing you later."

"Yes. Goodbye, Tyler."

He turned, visibly catching himself again. "This is inappropriate, but I'm going to ask it anyway. It is *Ms.* Greer, isn't it?"

He was right. The question was completely inappropriate. "Yes, it is. I'm…widowed." Well, murmuring that little tidbit was a shock, too. She didn't talk about her personal life to anyone. Certainly not to employees.

Certainly not to employees of mere minutes.

But Tyler's posture didn't give any indication that he thought things were maybe a bit too personal between them at all. Concern brushed over his features, making his eyes look far older than his years. "I'm sorry. Was your husband's passing recent?"

"Three years ago. Why?"

"I could say no reason, but since I've already dug myself a hole, I guess I'll go ahead and finish it. You're very attractive."

"I'm forty. Two." Covering her mouth with a cough, she tried again. "I mean, I'm forty-two."

He smiled. "Glad to know it. Have a nice day, Remy. And thanks for the job," he drawled over his shoulder as he walked out of the office.

Glad to know it? Thanks for the job? The minute he disappeared, she sagged against the wall.

And as soon as she closed her door, Remy rushed to the small refrigerator hidden in her back closet, opened a Perrier and chugged it back. She really needed to cool off.

Too bad the icy drink didn't help one bit.

"TYLER, ARE YOU SURE you know what you're doing?" Keith said as they sat on the edge of his dock and pretended to fish. "In the past six months you've quit your job, moved to Florida from Houston, sold your sprawling house and bought a dinky condo in Bishop's Gate."

His brother-in-law had summed up his life in one sentence. Now, that was pretty pathetic. "Thanks for the update. And yes, I do know what I'm doing."

"I don't think so. I can't believe you just took a call-center job at Carnegie. Are you going through a midlife crisis?"

"If it's midlife, it doesn't sound too promising for my life expectancy. I'm only thirty-four."

"Your age makes it all the more puzzling. Don't get me wrong—Cindy's thrilled her twin brother's finally close by. It's just that none of these actions seem like you."

They weren't. Slowly he tried to explain, though Tyler wasn't sure if any justification would ever be enough. "Ever since our parents died while we were in college, it's just been Cindy and me. When she found you and got married, I concentrated on work. Over the past six years, all I've done is live and breathe for my job. The morning you called to tell me Cindy almost died while she was in labor with April Marie, I was devastated."

"Feeling that way was only natural, Ty. It was scary."

"It was more than that. Keith, when April was born, I realized I'd never even laid eyes on Megan. I'd hardly seen Cindy at all. My priorities were completely screwed up."

"You've been working. She understood that."

"I didn't." Tyler leaned back to the soft-sided electric-blue cooler and pulled out another pair of beers. "Ten years of my life had gone by and I was as far away from your situation as possible. No wife, no family, no real ties. I want those things. I mean to have them."

"Okay. I can get you needing a change of venue. But Ty, a *call center?* It's going to be a drag."

"I've got my reasons for wanting to be there."

"Such as?"

"Nothing you need to worry about. Remember, I don't want a career right now. All I want is to be able to see my sister and my nieces and fish in the afternoon. And maybe one day find someone to settle down with."

"How are you going to find Ms. Right working in a cubicle?"

"Maybe I'll get lucky. There are a lot of women there."

His brother-in-law looked about to argue that point when Cindy called from the house. "Keith, can you help with the baths?"

"I've been summoned," he said, not looking as if he minded one bit.

Tyler supposed that Keith could truly understand what

it felt like, wanting a break from the constant traveling. A pilot for Carnegie Airlines, he was in a plane all the time. But Tyler didn't think Keith understood what it was like to have nothing to come home to.

Traveling had a far different feeling when home was little more than just a state of mind. When Keith stood, looking at him a moment longer under the brim of his baseball cap, Tyler waved an arm. "Go on. Cindy's going to be mad if you don't get a move on. I'm going to sit awhile longer, if you don't mind."

"Take your time."

As Keith trotted up the wood planks to the back of his house, Tyler sipped his beer and finally let himself unwind a bit. Now that he was alone, he relaxed and thought again about the woman he'd met that afternoon.

Ramona Greer had been just as striking in person as she was in the photo in the Carnegie Airlines in-flight magazine. From the moment he'd seen her photo, with her long hair pulled up in a fluffy twist and her beautiful smile, he'd been attracted to her.

But when he'd looked at that photo more closely, he'd noticed her gray eyes looked sad, as if she was alone in the world. He suspected there was a story lurking there. And he'd begun to think of those eyes as something of a challenge. If he could make her smile again, it would do a world of good for him and for her. After all, he'd just spent a long time thinking only about sales figures and bottom lines.

The magazine's short bio about her had only piqued his curiosity.

He'd wanted to meet her just to see if Ramona Greer in person affected him the same way.

He hadn't been disappointed.

He'd had no difficulty getting an interview at Carnegie. And it had been just plain luck that she'd interviewed him. From what Shawn Wagner said, that was an unusual circumstance. Usually the staff in human resources or Ramona's office assistant did the interviews.

It also hadn't been difficult to discuss his job experience. But it *had* been difficult to act professional when Ramona—Remy—had been shifting in that chair and her skirt inched up.

And it had been difficult to seem interested in the position when all he wanted to do was talk to her about life and hobbies and her past. He'd wanted to get to know her.

And when he'd shaken her hand, he'd been tempted to hold it just a bit longer than necessary. Her skin had felt soft and cool, her bones small and so feminine. Her nails were long, carefully filed and painted a creamy pink. She had beautiful hands. Now that he knew for sure she wasn't married, he was going to bide his time. And then he was going to make his move. He wanted to get to know Remy Greer, and wanted to get to know her soon.

Chapter Two

"I finished all the performance evaluations for the week," Shawn said on Friday afternoon, just after one o'clock. "In addition, I met with three of our new phone representatives who've been having some trouble. I gave them a little coaching."

Remy was glad Shawn was doing so well in her new position at Carnegie. Just six months ago she'd been one of the several hundred call-center representatives they employed in the Destin office.

Now she was Remy's assistant. She helped Remy with phone calls and managerial duties and helped new hires and probationary employees. All this added responsibility suited Shawn well. She was flourishing, and it was great to see. "How did the coaching go?" Remy asked. "Were they receptive to your advice?"

"I think so." Shawn frowned. "I never knew how much of what I did was based on instinct. It's been hard to fully explain my reasons for doing some things."

"If anyone can do it, you can," Remy said, feeling more certain than ever that promoting Shawn had been the right thing to do. Shawn had a knack for helping customers, and her quick thinking and problem-solving capabilities were certainly impressive. But the best thing was her rapport with her coworkers—no one minded her giving them tips. That was a real gift. "I know I've heard from more than a few reps about how much you've helped them."

Shawn's expression softened. "Thanks for telling me that."

"It's my pleasure. It's the truth." Looking out into the large area on the first floor, Remy enjoyed the bird's-eye view—the maze of call representatives in cubicles. A low buzz slowly echoed its way upstairs, reminding her of bees.

And—not for the first time—she wondered how Tyler Mann was doing. She wasn't going to ask.

She didn't want to ask. But she had to know. "So… how are the new hires?"

"Pretty good, I think."

"There're four, right?"

"Yes. One's on a shift right now." Shawn flipped through a few papers, obviously looking at schedules. "Tyler Mann."

Ramona knew that. She'd seen him enter the building on one of the video monitors. And when she'd done a walk-through earlier, she'd heard that Texas drawl. Careful to keep her voice nonchalant, she said, "Do you think he's going to work out all right?"

"Definitely. Although sometimes I just can't see why he's here."

"He does seem overqualified. Does he seem… happy?"

Shawn's eyes widened. "Happy? Well, yes, he looks happy. I haven't really checked on his stats or talked to him much. I thought I'd better give him some time." Shawn flipped through her notebook with a frown. "Why? Is there something you're worried about?"

"No. Not at all. Forget I asked."

"Oh."

Shawn was still looking at her strangely, and Remy knew the reason. They were more than three hundred employees. Remy didn't usually know most of the representatives' names, let alone ask after them. "Hey, it's after one o'clock, Shawn. I know you put in extra hours this week. Why don't you head on home?"

"I couldn't," she said. But her eyes shone.

"Sure you can. Go home and see those four kids of yours. Is Eddie working?"

"Actually, he had second shift. He's due home right about now."

"Even more of a reason to leave, don't you think?" After a separation and a surprise baby, Shawn and her husband had recently gotten remarried.

Shawn closed her calendar. "In that case, I'll go ahead and take off."

"Have a nice weekend," Remy said as Shawn practically raced out the door, closing it firmly behind her.

Then the silence felt deafening.

There were a thousand things to do. Unfortunately, she didn't want to do any of them. Feeling restless, Remy slipped on her black pumps, took the back stairs down to the floor and went for a walk.

After visiting with half a dozen people and smiling at a few others, Remy found herself standing at the entrance to Tyler's area, listening to him talk to a customer while capably checking flight schedules on his computer.

He certainly did seem competent. Easy. Not flustered. Nothing like how she was feeling.

He swiveled his chair her way the moment he hung up. And greeted her with a thousand-watt smile. "Hey, Remy."

"Hi. I just thought I'd stop by to see how you were doing."

He stood up, illustrating just how good a man could look in jeans and worn boots. "About as good as you can imagine for the first week." A dimple showed.

Now, that wasn't fair. Did he have to look so cute—and so incredibly young—all at the same time? She fought to keep a professional distance. "Well, that's good to hear. Just let Shawn know if you have any questions or concerns. She's the liaison and day-shift manager."

He sat back down and adjusted his headset. "I'll be sure and do that. Thanks."

Remy gave him a half smile and moved on. Because it wouldn't do to ask him out. Or to stand there talking about nothing for everyone to see. But as she heard him take a call, she couldn't help but listen to his deep voice. Couldn't help but hear the smile in it as he redirected the caller to another department.

Couldn't help but imagine how that Texas drawl would melt her insides if they just so happened to be sitting across from each other in a romantic restaurant.

Just as that vision raced across her mind, she stopped and shook her head to clear it.

Where had that come from?

Gosh, it had been ages since she'd thought about romantic restaurants or things like that. Years.

Practically a lifetime.

Chapter Three

Ah, the weekend. Tyler was so ready for it. Sitting in that cramped cubicle day after day was for the birds. So was talking to dozens of people who couldn't be ruder. He made a mental note to be a whole lot kinder to people in service jobs in the future. He was living proof that customer service reps definitely did not get the respect they deserved.

Getting the runaround all day sure made a guy want to do things differently. Sitting in the cubicle like an animal didn't sit too well with him. He was growing restless, especially since his whole reason for taking the job was to see Ramona Greer. So far, the only time he'd chatted with her was when she'd taken a tour and had briefly stopped by his desk.

Though the thirty-nine hours and fifty-five minutes of his first work week blended together in one horrible mishmash of regulations and hurried phone calls, he remembered each of those three hundred seconds in her company with extreme clarity.

She had such pretty eyes.

He had ached to pull down her hair, bunched in that fussy clip, just to see how long it actually was. Her suit fitted her perfectly, showing off a splendid set of calves.

He snorted. *Calves?* Who the hell thought about calves? Most women he'd dated in Houston showed a whole lot more leg in the middle of winter.

So had Kaitlyn, who worked in the cubicle right next to him. Every time he stood up, he'd been uncomfortably aware that she was eyeing him with interest. Kaitlyn was pretty. She had a great figure. She was probably a couple of years younger than he was and had taken pains to make sure he knew that she was available. Extremely available.

But Tyler wasn't even remotely interested.

Slipping his sunglasses back over his eyes, he got out of his Corvette and, with list in hand, prepared to get his errands done as quickly as possible. Keith and Cindy had invited him over for steaks and corn and fishing. He couldn't wait to gaze out at the greenish-blue waters of the Gulf and breathe fresh air.

The grocery store was handled easily enough. He made it in and out of the dry cleaner in record time. But, as usual, he couldn't seem to get out of Movies and More without buying a handful of DVDs.

It had always been like that. He liked to watch whole television series, one episode after another. Lately he'd become a fan of *Bones* and early seasons of *ER*. He didn't have a lot of vices, so purchasing a whole season at a time instead of renting episodes didn't really bother him.

He was just wondering if he should give *The Closer* a try when he spied the object of his affections right there on the other side of the aisle.

Remy.

Her hair was still pinned up. Didn't she ever wear it down? But that was where the similarities between her office look and weekend appearance ended. Obviously she'd stopped by her home before shopping. Gone was her usual suit. Instead, she had on khaki cotton shorts, a crisp black sleeveless blouse and low-heeled strappy black sandals. All that silky skin on display made his mouth go dry. And he'd thought those calves were something special! Those arms of hers were long and slightly toned. Completely feminine.

Arms? Lord, he had it so bad.

Remy was holding up an old Steve McQueen movie— *The Great Escape.* And then, as if sensing him, she looked up. Tyler could almost see her pupils dilate as she recognized him. "Tyler."

"Hey, Remy." He strode over. Motioning to the DVD she was holding, he said, "I never pictured you as a war movie fan."

"War movie?" She looked at the box in confusion before hugging it to her chest. "Oh, I like all kinds of movies."

"Me, too." He wondered if she was choosing a war movie because there was a man in her life. Didn't most women lean toward *Sex and the City* or something if they were sitting home alone? That's what Cindy said she watched.

She glanced at the box he held in his hand. "I like *The Closer.*"

"I've never seen it."

"You'll enjoy it. Everyone on the show is great." She paused and looked down. Her cheeks were stained red when she met his gaze again. "Well, I, uh, better get going."

No way did he want to let her go just yet. "So are you planning to watch that movie by yourself?" He stepped a little closer, just because he really wanted to. "On a Friday night?"

"No."

"Oh. Well, good." Shoot. Now he felt like the biggest fool imaginable. Here he was, making a play for his boss in the middle of the movie store. She probably had a great guy waiting at home for her. Or waiting at his house, anxious for her to come over and cuddle on the couch. "I won't keep you, then," he said. "Have a good weekend."

"You, too, Tyler."

He watched as she paid for the movie and strode out of the store, never once looking his way again. Obviously he was long forgotten.

Thinking quickly, he walked over and picked up a copy of the latest children's movie. If he couldn't spend the evening flirting with his boss, he might as well spend it eating chicken fingers with his nieces.

The kid at the cash register scanned his purchases. "That's forty-eight dollars, sir."

Tyler handed him a credit card, signed the receipt and got out of there. Just in time to see Remy Greer exit the parking lot in a nifty navy convertible, her hair contained in a cream-colored silk scarf. Oh, she was so pretty.

Oh, he had it so bad.

Remy loved her house. Mark had paid too much for it, but the location was amazing. Situated almost directly on the beach in a secluded inlet, the modern structure provided a calm and relaxing place for her to unwind after stressful days.

But as she entered her home and looked around at the modern paintings and Italian marble flooring, all she felt was cold.

Seeing Tyler Mann in the movie store probably did

that to a person. He'd caught her off guard, standing there on the other side of the aisle, smiling at her the way he always did. Talking to her in the sexy Texas drawl in a way that made her toes curl.

When she'd first seen him, she'd been so flustered, she'd picked up the first thing she could—some old war movie—and at his approach had hugged it tight as if it was her new best friend.

And then, of course, she'd made things even more uncomfortable by lying to him and saying she was definitely not going to be watching the movie alone. Yeah, right.

"Señora Greer, you're home early today," Carmen Rodriguez, her housekeeper of five years, said with a smile when Remy entered the vast kitchen filled with expensive stainless steel appliances that she rarely used.

"I am, for once. How are you?"

Carmen shrugged. "Fine. I made you some chicken and rice with some chilis."

"That sounds great. Thanks."

Still rubbing a spot on the black granite countertop that had already vanished, Carmen said, "Would you like me to serve you some dinner now?"

"No. I'll get some in a while."

"Oh. Well, all right." Then, brightening, Carmen walked over to the phone and picked up a slip of paper. "Oh, *senora,* I almost forgot. You received a message today from Señor Greer's mother. She says she's come back from her cruise."

Remy loved Linda Greer. She'd been a wonderful mother-in-law, and Remy was grateful that Linda still took the time to keep in touch even though it had been years since Mark had passed away. "How did she sound?"

"Good. I think she wants to see you." Carmen looked at Ramona with more than a hint of curiosity. "Are you ever going to date again, Señora Greer?"

Was nothing private anymore? "I don't know."

"You are a beautiful woman, and young, too," she said in what had to be the same way she talked to her seven grandchildren. "It's a shame to always be alone."

"It hasn't been that long."

Carmen shook her head. "Three years is long. It's been long enough, I think. You should be going out and having fun sometimes." A look of distaste crossed her features as she noticed Remy's infamous movie. "Not eating alone with war for company."

"Thanks for caring." Reaching out, she clasped her housekeeper's hand. Carmen had been so supportive while Mark had suffered through months of chemotherapy and then months in the hospital fighting a cancer that had ultimately won. She'd helped her learn to get out of bed when grief had turned her world black.

She'd stood by her side when Remy had cleaned out Mark's side of the closet, had made sure everything in her life ran like clockwork.

Carmen looked her over from head to toe, then shook her head. "I care, Señora Greer. But you need to care, too. What you need is a nice young man. Someone to make you smile again." She tapped her chest, right over her heart. "Someone to make you smile inside. Some romance, yes? Then you'll be happy again."

Oh, if Carmen only knew that just recently she'd been thinking the very same thing.

Chapter Four

"So Tyler, let me get this straight," Cindy said, her eyes shining as they sat in her darkened living room. "You have a crush on a woman. At your age."

"Yes, at my age. And might I remind you that it's your age, too?" Unsettled by her amused tone, he added, almost as an afterthought, "And what is wrong with thirty-four, anyway?"

"Nothing." She blushed. "I just think this crush is a little odd, Ty. I mean, she's your boss, she's a lot older, she's widowed—"

"She's not that much older, and she's only my boss because I've had to find a way to be near her."

"But still…she is a widow."

"Oh, come on. Everyone has a past, Cindy."

She kept talking as if he hadn't even spoken. "Most of all, she only thinks of you in terms of how many phone calls you complete per hour."

Remembering how flustered Remy always looked around him, he jumped at the chance to correct his sister's latest statement. "Remy thinks of me in other ways. I'm sure of that."

Instead of looking relieved, his sister just glowered. "Oh, I bet she does. I bet she's pleased she's got a new boy toy."

"Shut up, Cindy."

Immediately she winced. "You're right. I'm sorry I said that. But Tyler, I don't get it."

"I don't get it, either." He shrugged. "Your husband thinks I'm having a midlife crisis. He might be right."

"Yeah?"

"Yeah. Hell, I don't know. Or maybe not. Maybe meeting this woman was meant to be. Because all the points you're making are exactly right. On paper, she is wrong for me."

"But…?"

"But I don't care." Tyler smiled at his twin fondly. This was what he missed. Only Cindy would always carefully weigh everything he said as if it had merit. Only Cindy would listen to him admit that he'd been practically stalking Remy Greer and not laugh in his face.

Well, not completely laugh in his face. She was plenty amused, though.

"I see." For a moment Cindy said nothing, choosing instead to look out the window, where it was so dark only a few faint lights from fishing boats sparkled. Clouds had blown in that afternoon, and the weathermen predicted showers for most of Sunday.

He'd elected to spend the night at Cindy and Keith's instead of going home to his empty place.

"Actually, Tyler, now that I think about it—maybe what you're doing isn't so weird, after all. In some ways, it's vintage Tyler."

"In what way?"

"You've always been forceful and driven when you wanted something."

Ironically, he now felt like playing devil's advocate.

"Cindy, I saw Remy's photo in a magazine and I'm pursuing her. Who does that?"

"You." She giggled. "I wish I could have seen that interview. I wish I could have heard you chat about airline calls while staring at your girl."

"She's not my girl." He shook his head. "Plus, she's not a girl. She's a woman."

"A woman, huh?" Cindy's grin widened. "Wow."

He slumped against the couch. "I've got it so bad."

"That's the first step, right? Admitting the problem?"

"It's not a problem. I am going to ask her out."

"When are you going to do that?"

"I don't know. As soon as I figure out who she's watching war movies with."

"Maybe she's got a brother."

"Maybe." He stretched, feeling that their conversation had run its course. "What time is it?"

"I don't know. Sometime after midnight."

"I better let you get to bed. Those girls will be up with the sun in six hours."

"I don't care. Keith said he'd get up with them. You've got to know how much I'm loving our late-night chat. It reminds me of when we were in high school."

Tyler thought it was a little too much like high school. "It feels a little weird to me."

"I'm serious. A late night for Keith is bed at ten-thirty."

"Yet another reason to be glad we're twins. I don't know anyone else who has our crazy sleep schedule."

"I wonder who we got it from. Mom or Dad?"

The mention of their parents never failed to make a lump form in his throat. "I don't know. I do remember them hanging out in the family room, but never how late they stayed up."

A melancholy look appeared on Cindy's face. "Oh, they loved to sip wine and read mysteries."

"They were good together. I guess it's good in a way that they died together in that car accident. One would have been miserable without the other."

"You're right. They were two peas in a pod." She held out her hand and gripped his palm hard when he curved his fingers around hers. "But still...I would have liked even one of them to see my girls. Even after all this time, I still miss them."

"I do, too." Funny how *miss* never seemed like a strong enough verb. He ached for things that never were. That never had been. They simply hadn't had enough time with their parents.

"I don't know where I'm going with Remy. I don't know if anything will ever happen. But Cindy, I do know I need to at least try."

"I know." Slowly she got up and tossed the green blanket she'd been using on the back of the denim couch. "Well, I better get on up to bed. I think your room is all set."

"I promise I'll be fine. Go on to bed, Cin. See you in the morning." Tonight he was going to be sharing the baby's room. It had a daybed in the corner—a perfect size for Cindy...a tighter fit for him. But the company more than made up for the cramped conditions. Whenever he woke up, he loved hearing April suck her thumb and snore.

A half hour later, when he crawled under the sheets and heard April's steady breathing, Tyler sighed in contentment. He was so glad he'd gotten his priorities back in order. It still broke his heart that he'd missed so much of Megan's babyhood.

But as he drifted off to sleep Tyler couldn't help wishing that he was sharing a room with a different girl. One with lovely gray eyes and gorgeous ivory skin.

He wondered how she'd sound, sleeping next to him.

Sleeping? Since when had he thought about a woman he was attracted to sleeping? He should be picturing her naked in his arms. Oh, he had it so bad.

THE WEEKEND HAD BEEN never-ending. Carmen was right. She needed something else. She needed life and romance and light. Remy knew what she had now was only memories. And, well, that couldn't get a girl very far on a lonely Saturday night.

"You're here early," Shawn said, interrupting her train of thought.

"I could say the same about you. Shawn, it's only eight-thirty."

"I know." Looking shamefaced, she said, "I came in early because I was hoping you wouldn't mind if I left at one o'clock again today."

"Is everything okay?"

A faint blush covered her assistant's cheeks. "Yes."

"Oh. Well, then—"

"All four kids will be gone this afternoon. Eddie and I can have the whole house to ourselves."

"Ah."

Shawn plopped onto the seat. "You don't know what it's like, trying to get alone time, Ramona. None of the kids nap at the same time. Shoot, the oldest gave up napping years ago. And that baby…" She waved her hands in dismay. "Boys are a whole lot different than girls, let me tell you. Christopher is everywhere!"

Remy did her best to look serious, because Shawn certainly was acting as if she was in crisis mode. "Shawn, I definitely think you need to leave at one o'clock today."

"Thanks." She turned, took two steps, then turned around again. "I'm not going to make a habit of this. I promise."

She didn't want to make a habit of making love to her husband? If Shawn and Eddie just hadn't gone through a difficult separation, Remy would be tempted to tell her that she didn't know how lucky she was.

But she was pretty sure Shawn did know—and that was why she was taking time off to be with her husband. "Don't worry about leaving. Everything will be fine."

When Shawn opened the door, Remy caught a glimpse of someone very tall, dark haired and good-looking sitting on one of the chairs across from her assistant's desk.

Faster than his Corvette could accelerate, her pulse went into overdrive. "Tyler?"

Shawn looked at him in surprise. "Hi there, Tyler. Did we have an appointment I forgot about?"

Tyler stood up. "No. Actually, I'm here to see Ms. Greer."

To Remy's dismay, Shawn went all protective, stepping to the left and effectively blocking his way—and Remy's view.

Damn!

"I'm sorry, but Ms. Greer doesn't see people without appointments," Shawn said, all cool professionalism. And all business. "I'm sure I can help you with any problems you might be having."

"I'm not having problems."

"Then what—"

"I'll see him, Shawn. Thanks."

Sheer confusion filled Shawn's gaze as she stepped away from the door. Tyler strode right on through as Remy walked around her desk—around Mark's old desk—and met Tyler halfway.

For a split second his gaze flickered to her mouth and he leaned a bit closer. Then he stopped himself and relaxed his stance. "Thank you for seeing me."

"That's why I'm here." Over Tyler's shoulder Shawn was staring at the two of them, her eyes darting from one to the other. Because she was the boss, Remy did the only thing she could—she shut the door. Almost immediately the tension in the room increased.

Tyler smiled.

Chapter Five

Tyler made no move to sit down. Instead, he simply stood there, legs slightly spread apart, hands shoved into his pockets. Looking directly at her. Making her feel a tiny bit vulnerable. And—somewhat ironically—completely feminine.

Remy had no experience feeling like this. Usually she was the one in control in the room. She was the one who called the shots.

She never thought too much about that—it just was what it was. Well, it was that way after a few years of wearing suits, heels, minimal makeup and working longer hours than anyone else. Through it all she'd attained an aura of power—which, she imagined, was no different from the way men felt as managers in other companies.

But at the moment Tyler Mann didn't look as if he'd gotten that memo. The one that said she was all business and deserved a healthy dose of respect. He wasn't taking a single one of her nonverbal cues. Or looking to her for direction.

No, there wasn't a thing the slightest bit submissive in his body language. It was slightly disconcerting.

It was incredibly attractive.

She strove to retain the upper hand. Slipping her glasses on, she asked, "What may I help you with?"

He rolled back on the pads of his feet. "I stopped by to ask you a question."

He sounded as if he'd just wandered over to her house to borrow eggs. What he'd done was far different. His "stopping by" meant he'd left his cubicle, climbed the staircase and entered the executive office suite—unannounced and uninvited. "What do you need to know?"

Amusement flickered in his eyes as he stepped a little closer. Oh, he was tall. She was tall herself—almost five foot eight. He was at least six inches taller than that. "Actually, I wanted to know if you were dating anyone."

A thread of warmth snaked through her at his question. She fought it off with clipped words. "That question is completely inappropriate."

Instead of being cowed, he shrugged. "I know."

"I believe I told you that I'm a widow."

"I remember." His voice softened. "He's been gone what, three years?"

For some unknown reason, she just kept talking. "Yes. Three years."

"Have you dated since?" Tyler was close enough to touch. Close enough for her to smell his cologne. Close enough for her to see that he had a faint scar over one of his eyebrows.

No. No, she hadn't dated much. She hadn't even thought about it—well, not more than in the vague, philosophical sense. The fact that she was thinking about dating now—dating him—made her extremely nervous.

It was time to go on the offensive again. "Why are you asking?"

For a moment his dark eyes widened, as if she'd completely taken him by surprise. "Because I'm trying to ask you out."

"Trying?"

He grinned. "Obviously I'm not doing a very good job."

She stated the obvious. "You're an employee."

"I know." He shifted his weight, causing Remy's eyes to once again drift along his body. Today he was wearing a crisp white button-down with the collar buttons undone. Tanned skin peeked at her from his neck. Soft khakis and a wide dark leather belt showed he had no hidden beer belly. He was totally, completely attractive.

"I don't date employees."

"It's not against the law." A smile flashed. "I read the handbook."

"I'm not the law, Tyler. Merely your manager." She swallowed. "And I don't date coworkers."

"Why don't you make an exception?"

"I can't."

"Sure you can." A dimple appeared, making him look almost boyish. "Give a guy a break and say yes. You know, it took a lot of nerve to climb those stairs and come in here."

She doubted it. He seemed to have gumption to spare. "It's not a good—"

He interrupted. "I thought we could go sailing."

"Sailing?"

"Uh-huh." With one swoop, he seemed to take in her black suit and high heels. "Say yes."

"I've never been sailing." Against her will, visions of herself on the deck of a sailboat, wind in her hair, bright white sails standing tall overhead, flew into her mind.

"Then it's time you went, don't you think?"

More pictures appeared. Tyler bracing himself by sliding two hands on either side of her body. She, resting against that chest. Forgetting about everything except the sun and the sea and the way the air felt crisp and clean.

But she couldn't. What would everyone say if they saw the two of them together? What would Mark have thought? "I'm sorry. No."

Breaking the spell, he stepped back. "Remy, be honest. Is it me, or is it the job?"

It was both. Plus more. It was her. It was the things she was feeling that felt scary and forbidden. "I don't date, Tyler. But if I did, I would never date someone who worked for me."

"You know I'm going to ask again. I don't give up easily."

"No, I don't imagine you do." With a sigh, she did what she had to do. "I'm sorry, but if you are working today, I do believe your break is over."

Within four steps, he'd opened her door, then walked out, never once looking back. Remy closed the door again before Shawn could even think about darting in and asking what was going on.

But as Remy leaned back against the wood, she noticed—with some surprise—that her hands were shaking.

KAITLYN SINCLAIR HAD never gone to college. Right after high school she'd attended nine months of beauty school. But somehow, right in the middle of perms and relaxers, she'd had an epiphany. No way on earth was she going to spend the rest of her days sticking her hands into someone else's hair.

Tyler found all that out during the five minutes it took to get to the employee parking lot at seven o'clock Friday night.

"So that's how I ended up at Carnegie," she said, her blond hair swinging with each step. "Answering phones is a lot easier than cutting hair."

"I imagine so. I mean, here, all you have to do is talk. A lot."

"That part's easy for me. I've never minded talking on the phone. In fact, some people have said that talking is one of the things I do best."

Tyler mentally rolled his eyes. Since she sat next to him in cubicle world, he knew exactly how much she talked on the phone. Incessantly. Kaitlyn talked loudly and forcefully. To customers. To her mother. To her roommate, Teresa. "Well, hope you have a good weekend."

She flipped her hair back, and her hair fell over one shoulder like a curtain made of liquid gold. "A bunch of us are going to Bishop's Pub for happy hour. Why don't you join us?"

"Thanks, but I've already got plans."

"Oh." Lashes batted. "Do you have a date?"

Did a date with a two-year-old count? At the moment, absolutely! "Yeah. I promised someone I'd take her fishing. Sorry."

"Fishing? Oh. Sure. No problem."

With a wave, Tyler clicked open the lock on his car, then sank into the camel leather. About a dozen cars over, Kaitlyn got in and drove off in her spiffy red Chevy Malibu. Thinking again of her offer, Tyler called himself a fool.

Her offer had been genuine and sweetly made. Over

the years he'd dated plenty of women who weren't as sweet or as pretty.

And beneath that somewhat dim, nonstop talking, there was probably a woman with a good heart lurking. After all, she did call her mother several times a day. Perhaps she'd be great wife material when she matured a bit.

And, well, she definitely found him attractive. She'd smiled, flirted and touched his arm every time they talked.

But he'd bet money that she didn't find him half as attractive as he found Ramona Greer. Lord, he didn't know what it was about those silk blouses of hers, but every time he saw her he couldn't help but imagine making love to her with just one of those shimmery garments on...and slowly coming off.

So far, his favorite was the black blouse with the little keyhole collar. On Kaitlyn, it would look demure, almost nunlike.

On Remy, it made her gray eyes look even more luminous and her beautiful ivory skin glow.

He'd just turned on the ignition when his cell phone rang. Seeing that it was his sister, he answered immediately. "Hey, Cindy. I'm on my way over."

"You might want to rethink that. Megan's got the stomach flu."

"Guess that fishing trip is going to have to wait."

"I'm afraid so." She sounded worried.

"I'm about to pull out of the parking lot. Do you need anything?"

"Actually, I do. Ty, would you please run by the drugstore and pick up some baby Motrin? I hate to ask, but Keith is gone and I just can't take Megan anywhere."

"Of course you can't. What else do you need?"

"Pedialyte and maybe a coloring book. And a bottle of wine. Red."

Shifting into First, he smiled as he pulled out of the parking lot. "Megan's that bad, huh?"

"She's already ruined two carpets. I'm going to have to call the carpet cleaners. But don't worry. I'm not going to make you even step inside."

Tyler knew this was just one of the many things his sister had been dealing with for the past few years. A husband who constantly traveled and no family around to lend a helping hand. Guilt for never even imagining her trials swung forward, making him realize once again that he'd made the right choice when he decided to come to Florida.

Though he was man enough to admit that being around a pukey two-year-old might be pushing his uncle limits a bit far. "What about the baby?"

"April's great. Right now I'm trying to keep them away from each other. It's a nightmare, though, because you know how April likes to be rocked."

"How about I take her for the night?"

"What?"

Warming up to the idea, he said, "I'm no mom, but I can take care of a baby. For one night, at least."

"Ty, there's a car seat involved. And bottles and diapers! I can't even believe I'm thinking about this."

"I'll take your car. Pack up a bag for April and we'll do a trade when I get there."

"Ty—"

"That way you can get some rest when Megan does. Keith's not due home tonight, is he?" Tyler seemed to recall he was flying overseas this week.

"No. I'm on my own until Monday morning."

She sounded exhausted. "It's settled. Pack me a bag,

Cindy. Actually, pack more than you'd ever think April will need."

"Are you sure?"

He was sure. "I love you, too, Cindy."

"Thanks."

"Anytime. See you soon." Well, it wasn't drinks with Kaitlyn, but it was still spending the night with a blonde, Tyler mused. Plus, in his opinion, little tiny April, with her perfectly cute toes and gummy grin, was far preferable. Even better, she hardly spoke a word.

TWO HOURS LATER, when he crossed paths with Remy at Movies and More, searching for a movie that might lull April to sleep, he almost laughed out loud at his good fortune.

Luckily, Remy looked as if she couldn't help smiling at their meeting either. "We have to stop meeting like this." Then, when she saw he was holding a very cute six-month-old in one arm, her eyes widened and her expression faltered. "I didn't know you had a baby."

"I don't. This is my niece April. I'm babysitting tonight. My sister's other kid is sick with the flu."

Yearning and sweetness transformed Remy's features. Reaching out, she touched one of April's tiny feet. "Oh, Tyler. She's adorable. Look how cute these little socks are!"

"Every bit of her is cute." Giving in to temptation, he gave the baby a little squeeze and a gentle kiss on top of her wispy curls. Ty was pleased to see April was doing her part to be as irresistible as ever. At the moment she was simply staring at Remy with a pair of beautiful blue eyes.

Still playing with April's foot, Remy asked, "Do you watch your niece often?"

"No. This is my first overnight. My brother-in-law, who's a pilot, is out of town. My sister, Cindy, sounded so tired, I decided that the least I could do was help out a little."

"That's sweet of you."

"It's probably pretty dumb—she might end up crying all night. But we'll see. My car is packed with April supplies. But then I remembered that she likes baby DVDs, so I thought I'd pick up the newest one."

"Good luck." She held out her hand. "Can I help you carry the DVDs or something? Your arm's got to be wearing out, holding that baby."

"I'll take the help," he said, handing her a Baby Einstein DVD and two comedies. Then, because he couldn't resist, he added, "It's a good thing you ended up saying no to sailing. I would have had to cancel on you."

"I guess everything was meant to be."

Because she looked so entranced with April, he pushed a bit. "I'm just going to be sitting at home tonight, watching baby movies and ordering pizza. Is that enough to tempt you to come over?"

"Oh." Letting go of April's foot, Remy straightened. "I'm sorry, but I don't think so."

"Are you saying no because we work together? How about if I promise I won't tell a soul at Carnegie that I saw you outside of those hallowed halls?" Lowering his voice, he added, "Plus, it's not even really a date. It's babysitting."

For a moment Tyler was sure she was going to cave in. Longing flooded her gaze…though whether it was for him or little April he didn't know. But he had a pretty good idea that the way to any woman's heart was a baby. "Please? I'm sure you know a lot more about babies than I do."

"Actually, I don't. I...I don't know a thing about them. I'll just help you to the counter before I go."

"But you haven't picked out a movie yet." Her hands were clutching his movies as if they were about to slip away. "We're in no hurry. Why don't you look around for a minute and then we'll leave together?" And then he could coax her one more time to hang out with him for a while.

"I'm not going to get anything. I don't know why I even came in here." Before she even finished speaking, she turned and led him to the counter.

Unfortunately there were three cashiers open and waiting. The moment the kid started scanning his movies, Remy gave him a little wave. "Bye, Tyler."

"Hey, wait—"

But she was already gone. "Crap," he said.

"Ap!" April echoed.

"Dude, she left you high and dry," the cashier remarked as Tyler handed him his credit card.

Shifting April to his other hip, Tyler had to admit the kid was right. Once again Remy had left him, without so much as a backward glance.

Chapter Six

It was 3:00 a.m. and Remy was staring at the digital clock next to her bed again. Oh, she hated insomnia. Hated feeling so completely out of control with her body. No matter what she did, sleep wasn't going to happen.

Since she'd already been staring at the clock for an hour, Remy slipped on her robe. In the hall she felt at a loss. The kitchen was deadly for her in the middle of the night. Before she knew it, she would consume a bag of crackers without even realizing it. The television didn't sound inviting, either.

But did it ever in the middle of the night?

Finally giving in to that tiny inner voice she usually tried so hard to ignore, Remy opened the door to the guest bedroom.

As she knew they would, memories rushed forward.

When they'd first gotten married, the bedroom had held wedding presents. Later it served as her pride and joy for visiting relatives. Because the view was spectacular, she'd kept the room in shades of ivory and white, choosing to brighten it with gilded mirrors, sparkling shells and coral…and the haunting colors of the Gulf outside. When she came to visit, Mark's mom in particular loved to sit in bed and sip coffee while the sun rose.

For a brief time, she and Mark had entertained ideas about transforming the serene sanctuary into a baby dreamland. She'd always loved the idea of a *Jungle Book*-themed room for a little boy or girl. Something bright and cheerful and filled with stuffed animals.

And then she'd realized she couldn't have children.

Against her will, Remy breathed deeply and was flooded with memories, the kind that never seemed to completely fade and were brought forth with the tiniest of prompts. All of them involved Mark.

Sometimes it felt as if she remembered two Marks.

The man she'd married smelled like cologne and soap, and was full of laughter. He'd carried her into this room the day they'd moved in, laughingly saying that he intended to carry her over every threshold in the house.

Three years later the Mark who had rested in this room had been so very sick and thin. Frail. Dying.

The drapes were closed. Carefully Remy pushed the remote control that she'd had installed when it was too hard for Mark to get out of bed. After a moment's pause the curtains parted, revealing the tranquillity of the water outside.

Moonlight glimmered on the waves, illuminating the surf and a few oil rigs in the far distance.

With care, Remy sat in the hard wooden rocking chair that still perched on the bed's left side. The seat felt hard and familiar, the back sturdy and solid. It had been her spot.

Once Carmen had spoken about moving the chair. It was in the way, cluttered the room. It didn't go with the white woodwork and clean lines of the dresser. Remy couldn't bear to move it even an inch, and had told Carmen so.

Now, as she crossed her legs and tried to relax, Remy decided that maybe she wasn't quite as ready to move on as she'd supposed.

"I met a guy, Mark," she said to the empty room. "You wouldn't believe it. He's young. A pup, you would say." She almost smiled at the word. *Pup* had been Mark's favorite term for anyone a little too green.

"He flirts with me constantly. No, wait, that's not true. He flirts with me whenever we see each other, which isn't a lot. But he asked me out today. To go sailing, of all things!"

Of course, no one answered. But in her mind, Remy already knew what Mark would be saying. He'd had a quick, vibrant mind. If he'd been sitting in the bed, Remy knew he'd already be asking a million questions.

What's he like?

"He's young," she told the imaginary voice. "But he's not as green as I make him sound. He's had a whole career already, selling some kind of computer software. He did well in that field, too. I know, because I checked him out."

But now?

"Now he just wants a regular old job. I don't understand it, but he's adamant about it. I guess he missed his sister, and he wanted to be near her. And yes—before you ask—he's handsome. I'm talking really handsome. Like cover-model gorgeous."

Well, if she was going to reveal all her secrets, she might as well go in with both feet. "Mark, for a moment there, when he asked me out, I wanted to say yes. Sailing sounds like fun. Anything different does, you know? I mean, all I've done for the last three years is work."

Why didn't you go?

"Because I was afraid." She slumped, almost welcoming the hard wood against her head. "I was afraid if I said yes I'd be unfaithful."

You promised.

"That promise wasn't fair, Mark. You were dying." But, yes, she had promised to date again one day. To fall in love again one day.

But she really hadn't imagined such a thing possible.

Looking out Mark's window, gazing at the shadows of waves sparkling in the moonlight, Ramona felt at a loss as to what to do. "Actually, right now…I'm thinking that maybe if he asks again—if Tyler asks me out again—I'm going to say yes. I'm going to say yes, or shoot, I don't know. I'm going to get a kitten or something." Heaven knew she needed something to cuddle.

A cat? Hell, no.

Against her will, Remy laughed. Mark had always hated cats. And then, just as she was laughing at herself, the chair creaked. Hastily she jumped to her feet. For a moment she'd been afraid the whole thing was going to fall apart right under her.

Stunned, she stared at the chair. "Well, if that's not symbolic, I don't know what is. All right, then. I will get up and do something. Even if it hurts.

"And, uh, Mark? I'll wait on the kitten, too. We both know Carmen would kill me. She's no fan of cats, either."

Fighting a yawn, she went back to bed, amazed that an hour had passed. When she slept, she dreamed of sailing…and of feeling happy and free.

"No, MA'AM. I'm sure I don't know what you're going through," Tyler said, each word feeling as if it was getting pulled through his gritted teeth. "However, I don't know what you want me to do about you missing the plane."

Oops. Wrong thing to say. In explosive terms, the cranky lady on the phone began to tell him exactly what he could do. None of it sounded humanly possible.

In his previous life he would have hung up on her. No, correction. In his previous life he would have told her exactly what he thought of her directives, and would have given her a few choice ideas to think about, too.

But now he was living at the bottom of the food chain, in the-customer-is-always-right world.

Except, well, she wasn't right. Mrs. Redding had overslept and missed her damn plane.

Fingers gliding over the keyboard, Tyler clicked on all available flights to Miami from Buffalo for the next twelve hours. "There's another flight in five hours. You'll arrive here at midnight."

"I'm going to miss my cruise."

"Then you should have either planned better or gotten out of bed," he snapped. A little too loudly.

Kaitlyn stood up and stared at him over the cubicle, waving her hands to grab his attention. *Stop,* she mouthed. *Be nice!*

But Kaitlyn's warning came too late. "I want your supervisor!" the woman screamed into his earpiece.

"No problem," he retorted. Then, without another word, he transferred her to Shawn.

"So, Tyler," Shawn said when he was called to her desk twenty minutes later—just like a cheater in grade school. "How do you think you could have handled Mrs. Redding's phone call in a better way?"

Standing in front of her, Tyler fought against the impulse to roll his eyes. "I could have tried harder to listen to her needs."

"Gee, that sounds almost like a textbook answer."

"Page five. I did read the manual."

She almost smiled. Almost. But then she leaned back in her chair and looked him over. "May I be frank?"

"Of course."

"You're a puzzle to me. You're definitely not the type of guy who looks used to dealing with irritating phone calls or irate customers. I don't understand why you're working here. Maybe we should rethink your position?" Opening a binder, she flipped a few bright orange tabs. "There might be something over at Corporate that might be better—"

No way was he getting out of this place. "I want to work here. On the phone."

"But you don't seem to really care—"

"Shawn, I care. I do," he said so quickly, so sincerely, *he* almost believed it. "Look, I lost my temper because a rude and obnoxious woman just chewed me out like I wasn't good enough to pick up her trash. I'm sorry. Next time she calls, I'll try to be nicer."

But instead of nodding and commiserating, Shawn narrowed her eyes. "Mrs. Redding won't be calling again. She told me she'd never fly on our airline again. Ever."

"I see." Well, that was no great loss. Shoot, the rest of the company ought to send him some champagne.

"Do you? Because in case you haven't heard, the airline industry is hurting and we can't afford to make customers mad. Not even the jerks." Leaning back, she tilted her head up to meet his eyes. "I told all of you in the training sessions that the best call representatives make our job look ridiculously easy. It's not. If you thought it was going to take the same skill as—" she paused for a moment, then lit on his phrase "—picking up trash, then you need to tell me now."

"I don't need to tell you a thing. What I should have done was explain to her about the penalties and calmly do my best to get her on the next available flight. And ignore her snide comments."

"Next time, please do that." After another moment she stood up and held out her hand. "Thanks for coming up."

"Thanks for letting me stay," he replied, shaking her hand with a smile.

Just as he was about to leave, Remy appeared on the stairs, her arms laden with file folders, a thin vase of red roses in one hand. Her arrival reminded him why it wasn't so bad to be at Carnegie. Why putting up with a dozen Mrs. Reddings a day was worth the irritation.

She paused when their eyes met. "Hi, Tyler. Is everything okay?"

"No. I snapped at a caller and have been getting chewed on a bit."

Remy looked alarmed. "Oh?"

"Don't worry." Shawn laughed. "I haven't been chewing on him all that hard. Although I should have."

"Did you get the customer's problem resolved?"

"As well as possible. She really was a witch," Shawn said with a grimace. "She was determined to make as many people as possible miserable in one phone call. She did a pretty good job, too."

Noticing Remy's full hands, Tyler stepped forward. "Do you need some help?"

Her cheeks flushed. "Thanks. These roses. I don't know what I was thinking...."

He did. She looked pretty carrying around flowers. If

she'd ever warm up to him, he'd send her some. He took the vase from her hand, then grabbed the key peeking out of her palm, clicked open her office door, flipped on the light and set the vase down on the edge of her desk.

Delighted that she'd allowed his help without complaint, he smiled her way. "I guess we're destined to be helping each other out, aren't we? You helped me carry DVDs at Movies and More, and now here I am, carrying your roses."

"It's almost a habit." She slid her hands down the sides of her navy pencil skirt. On some girls, the action would look incredibly suggestive. But he was learning enough about her now to know that it was nerves.

But still, he did enjoy watching her hands smooth the fine gabardine fabric over her thighs.

"So...how was April? Did she like the movie?"

"She loved it. I have to say I survived the night with only a half dozen moments of panic. But I'm a pro at diaper changing now. It's impressive."

"I am impressed."

He was pleased she was still standing close. That she looked happy to be talking to him. "So, how was your weekend?"

"Oh. Fine. Nothing special."

"Do you have plans for next weekend?"

"No. It's only Monday."

"Then make some. Come sailing with me on Saturday." He grabbed her hand when she looked about to refuse. "I know all your reasons for saying no. But I'd love it if you'd just say yes."

Her eyes widened. With her hand still locked in his she paused, and then...nodded. "Yes."

Tyler felt like laughing, he was so relieved. "Yes?

Really? Hey, that's great. Thank you. I'll talk to you later about when and where to pick you up."

"That's not necessary. I could easily meet you at the marina."

Still holding her hand, he looked at the way it looked so perfect nestled in his own. Thought about how slim her hands were. How soft and cool. "No, you couldn't. I pick up women for dates. Always."

For a moment her lips parted. For a second he spied her gaze center on his lips. Then she shook her head. "Well, then. All right. I will, ah, give you my address later."

"All right." He wanted to kiss her. He wanted to lean close and kiss those lips. Not anything much, just to touch her some more. Hell, he'd settle for her cheek. Something to show her that he was pleased.

But it was too soon. Even if he wasn't in his boss's office. Even if he hadn't just gotten his butt chewed by her assistant, it was too soon.

He settled for a gentle squeeze to her hand before finally releasing it. "I better go. I've got more phones to answer, you know."

She blinked. "About that phone call—"

"I'm going to be nicer. I promise. Bye, Remy."

Quickly he walked out into the hall and back down the stairs. Slid into his seat and slipped his headset back on. But just as he was about to click on to a call, a faint scent brought him to a halt.

He knew what it was the unmistakable aroma of freshly cut roses.

Chapter Seven

Carmen's face lit up as if it was Christmas Day when Remy walked through the kitchen door, arms laden with shopping bags from Destin Commons Mall. "Oh, Señora Greer! Have you been out shopping? For something other than work clothes?"

"I have." After setting two of the bags on the floor, she pulled out a pair of khaki shorts and a cherry-red T-shirt from the third. Holding them up in front of her, Remy said, "What do you think?"

"I am not sure." In her typical style of weighing every pro and con before saying a thing, she said, "Where are you going?"

"Sailing." Then, because she needed as much support as she could, Remy spit out the next part. "With a man."

A flash of color ignited her cheeks. "Oh, saints above. You're going on a date?"

"I am. Now, stop looking like you're about to break into song," Remy said sheepishly. Going out with another man was a big step. Going sailing—doing something out of her usual comfort zone—was a really big step.

Huge.

"I've got a date tomorrow morning. Tyler is picking me up at nine."

To Remy's surprise, Carmen plucked the outfit from her hands, flipped it over, examined it from all directions, then clucked a bit. "Yes, these are very nice but...I think they're too much."

"Too much how?"

"Well, I've never been sailing...." Carefully Carmen handed the shirt and shorts back. "Even I know sailing involves sun and the water. You should be wearing a bathing suit, yes?"

There was no way she was going to get that bare in front of him. Not Tyler. "I'm not wearing a bathing suit on a first date."

"Do you even have a bathing suit?"

"You know I do." Remy pointed to the lap pool adjacent to the lower-belevel deck. "You've seen me swim."

"In those black racing suits." Waggling her brows, she said, "You need something with a bit more color, I think. Like pink or green. And smaller. Like a bikini."

"I wouldn't know the first store to get a new bikini, even if I wanted to wear one, which I don't."

"There're two stores in the mall that have good deals," Carmen said. "I know—I took Bridget there on Monday night."

"Bridget's your granddaughter, Carmen!"

"There were women in there, too. Some who were far older than you, Señora Greer." Tapping her foot, her coral toenails with the tiny rhinestones glinting, Carmen caught Remy's eye. "You should go right back to the mall now. And get a halter-top style, too. Bridget says that is a good kind. On you, it would look *muy bueno,* I think."

"Carmen," she sputtered. "How come you know more about bikinis than I do? Is this all from Bridget?"

"I have Bridget, yes. But I've also been out, looking in stores. Watching Oprah and Regis and Kelly, too. You, Señora Greer, have been in hiding."

It felt that way. For a moment Remy was tempted to take every bit of advice that Carmen had spouted and run to the mall. But then, like an old friend, good old nerves and insecurities caught her again. What if Tyler didn't like what he saw?

What if she didn't like what she was showing him?

"I can't. Not yet." Picking up the shorts and T-shirt, she said, "I was thinking this would be a good first step. And I will take a bathing suit, just in case."

"Maybe so. Ah, well, next time, we'll show more skin."

"Next time." That was, if she could survive the first time. "I hope it goes okay. You know, I haven't been sailing in years. Not since Mark and I were newlyweds."

"Whatever you do will be okay if the company is good, yes?"

"Yes." This was why she admired Carmen so much. She had a way about her that was two parts sugar and one part salt and vinegar.

"So, what is he like, this Tyler?"

Young. That's what she wanted to say. But now that she knew him better, she knew that wasn't all he was. "He's handsome and nice. Listen to this. He watched his sister's baby last weekend because her other daughter had the flu. And he likes movies. I've seen him in the movie store twice now."

"Those are good things." Looking satisfied, Carmen walked over and picked up her purse and keys. "I made you a salad and some clam chowder for tonight."

"That sounds great. Thank you."

"You're welcome. You have a good time tomorrow, Señora Greer, and don't worry so much."

"I can't help it."

Seconds later Remy was enfolded in a generous hug. Patting her just as she probably did her own daughter, Carmen clucked. "Tomorrow night you will be glad you did something fun for a bit. This is called living, right?"

"Right."

"If you don't like this Tyler, don't see him again." She snapped her fingers for emphasis. "It's that simple."

Somehow Remy was afraid that wasn't going to be the case at all. She was afraid she was going to like him way too much. Way too much.

TYLER DECIDED Ramona's home looked like something out of *In Style* magazine. Sleek and modern, the sprawling ranch meshed completely with both the coastline it was situated on and the water it overlooked. Glass and chrome and green tile complemented one another, coaxing the observer's gaze to flicker from one window to the next.

It was impressive.

Somehow, though, he had thought she'd reside in a place a little more family-friendly. Something a little more relaxed and low-key. Looking around at the expensive landscaping, Tyler winced. Everything was so picture-perfect, it looked as if no one lived there.

He was eager to get Remy out of the office and out on the water. Anywhere they could relax and forget about Carnegie.

Remy opened the door mere seconds after he rang, her hair pulled up in a ponytail. She was dressed in a neat pair of shorts and red T-shirt. "You're right on time."

"Punctuality has always been a strong suit of mine," he murmured as he stepped into her marble entryway. He was teasing, of course—Tyler had never cared about being punctual. No, all he'd been thinking about was seeing her again.

Someplace he could be himself, where she could be herself. Not together as boss and subordinate.

But boy, did he love to flirt with her. Even the tiniest hint of a suggestive comment caused her to get flustered.

Just as she was right now.

Though he was tempted to tease her a bit more, just to see if she'd rub those hands down her thighs one more time, he was sure that wasn't the way to go. They had a whole day to spend together, and he wanted her to enjoy it as much as he knew he was going to.

Seeking now to put her at ease, he forced his eyes to look beyond her, to the open beauty of the living room and the balcony beyond. He whistled softly. "This place is amazing, Remy. Look at that view."

She led the way to a pair of white French doors that overlooked a large patio lined with several potted ferns and bougainvillea. "This view is one of my favorite things about the house. Nothing's more relaxing than gazing at the water."

"Did you build this place yourself?"

"No. Well, yes. I mean, Mark did."

"Your husband."

"Yes." Still looking out in the distance, she said, "I love this place, but it was the cause of a thousand fights." Turning to him, she shook her head with a small smile. "I'm more of a small-town gal at heart. At least, I thought

I was. I pictured living in a place that had neighborhood barbecues and sidewalks and cul-de-sacs. Not this."

"But now?"

"Now I appreciate the beauty, and I'm thankful for the privacy."

"It's private, all right." Stepping closer, he playfully leered at her. "If you wanted, you could sunbathe naked all day long. Ever done that?"

"Of course not! I don't—" Her eyes narrowed. "Oh, stop. I swear, you love to get me going."

"It's fun." When she returned his smile, he said, "You ready?"

"I think so." She ran her hands down her thighs. "So, is this okay?"

"It's more than okay. It's perfect."

"I wasn't sure if I needed a bathing suit. I thought I'd bring one."

"You can do that. Or put it on now. Whatever you want."

"I'll just take it. Oh! I cut up some vegetables and fruit."

"Great. I've got beer and soda and water. And there's a great restaurant nearby. The Silver Pelican."

"I've been there."

"Let's go, then, okay?"

Once again she led the way, stopping to lock the doors behind them before going back to the foyer. That's when he noticed a large canvas bag filled with enough towels and things to spend the weekend on the boat. "You know this is just for the afternoon, right?"

"Did I overpack?"

"Not for a weeklong cruise." Picking up the bag he gave a little grunt, just for show.

She saw it and frowned. "Sorry. I didn't know what

to bring…." She paused while slipping on a cute pair of white-and-navy deck shoes. "You're teasing me again."

"I am. I can't seem to help myself."

MOMENTS LATER they were on their way. Remy leaned her head against the headrest and smiled. "I feel more relaxed already."

To his surprise, Tyler realized that he, too, was relaxing. It came as a shock—he hadn't realized he had been on edge. But he would have been a fool not to have been.

This date was important to him, as was Remy's opinion about it. If things crashed and burned, there would never be a second date and he'd be stuck at Carnegie. Condemned to weeks of torture until he could either figure out a new way to win her over…or persuade himself to give up his dream.

In addition, he'd also been unsure about how she was going to act away from the office—and afraid that perhaps he'd just been imagining that there was more to the attractive woman by his side than the ability to look good in just about any style of suit.

He'd been worried she'd be stiff and want to talk only about work, which would have been laughable. He hated that job as much as she reveled in it. But, thankfully, all of his worries had been laid to rest. Instead of being a workaholic, from the moment she'd opened the door she'd acted like a girl. A pretty, endearing, adorable one.

Traffic was light. As they sped down the highway in the short track to the marina, he glanced her way again. Bold oversize sunglasses covered her eyes. Her pretty hands rested lightly on her uncrossed knees, almost as if she was sitting in church.

To him, she looked like an elegant woman, and he couldn't wait to know more about her. "Tell me about your family, Remy."

"My family? Hmm. Well, I have parents who still live in the same house where I grew up in Indiana and a brother who's in Kansas City."

"Are y'all close?"

"We were." She paused to consider. "Now, I don't know. I see them all once or twice a year. My brother's married and has four kids. My parents always prefer to go to his place for Christmas."

"You don't go there, too?"

"No. It's too—" She cut herself off. "I mean, Thanksgiving until New Year's is Carnegie's busiest time. I can't take time off. Imagine a dozen Mrs. Reddings an hour. It's exhausting."

It did sound painful. It also sounded like a lie.

There was something she wasn't telling him. Had she really been spending the past three years alone at Christmas? "What about Mark's family?"

"Oh, they live pretty close. In Pensacola, just an hour away. I see them some."

"But not often?"

"I used to." She paused before continuing. "Actually, not as much anymore. Time passes, you know."

He did know. The first few holidays without his parents had been especially difficult.

When he didn't reply right away, Remy continued. "See, seeing one another reminds us all of Mark's passing. He was our link, of course. Now it's like there's always an empty seat around us, though I'm sure they don't mean to make it seem that way. So, what about you?"

Saved by the parking attendant. "I'll have to fill you in on me later. We're here."

After pulling out her bag and his backpack, he led her across a grassy picnic area and then down to the rows of slips. Finally they stopped in 16C, the home of *Cynthia*.

"*Cynthia,* hmm? Who's she?"

"My sister."

She smiled. "You named your boat after your sister?"

"I didn't. My brother-in-law, Keith, did. It's his boat." Just to make her smile, he gave her a warning look. "So don't expect too much, sailingwise. I can sail, but I'm far from a pro."

To his surprise, Remy looked as if that was the best news, ever. "I'm glad. I was beginning to think there was nothing you couldn't do."

"Was that a compliment?"

"Maybe. You're one of the most confident men I've ever met."

Thinking about how much he wanted to pull her into his arms and claim her lips, he had only one reply. "Believe me, there's plenty I can't do. But I'm trying." After stepping on the deck, he held out a hand to help her in.

But then, on the spur of the moment, he switched strategies and curved his hands around her waist and pulled her up.

"Oh!" Remy's hands went to his shoulders. And then, because he couldn't resist, he swung her in a half circle and kissed her cheek when he set her down.

She gripped his shoulders to steady herself. "What was that for?"

"No special reason. I just wanted to say welcome aboard."

Pull your hands down, Remy cautioned herself. But her arms were in no hurry to listen, as they remained at his shoulders a few moments longer than necessary.

Tyler didn't look as if he minded, though. Something flashed in his eyes and his own hands curved around her waist a bit more.

Then, before she knew it, he lowered his head and kissed her. Touching her mouth this time instead of her cheek.

And then, before she could analyze that, he kissed her again. This time more softly. More slowly. She couldn't help but respond in kind. Tilting her head a bit, she kissed him back. Stepped a little closer.

Everything she'd ever imagined about him was true. His lips were firm and gentle, his touch languid and assured.

Tyler Mann was a guy who knew how to kiss.

With a mumble of appreciation, he opened his lips. Remy did the same. And then things just went on and on.

Oh, what a kiss. Maybe it lasted two minutes. Maybe just two seconds, but when he raised his head, Remy knew that she'd be thinking about it now every time she looked at him.

She could admit that she enjoyed looking at him, too. He was handsome, and the way he wore his clothes suggested that he had a stylist or something.

Everything about his look just fit him. Tyler wore flip-flops, long khaki shorts and a stark white T-shirt that set off his tan. His sunglasses were attached to a short cord around his neck, so they hung around his collar.

The young clothes fit him, fit his style. Yep, all of him radiated fitness and success and health.

So different from the way Mark had appeared in his last year.

As those painful images threatened, she blinked hard. She wasn't going to go there. Not today.

"So…what can I do to help?"

He handed her the tote. "Take this belowdeck and then come join me back up here." He motioned to a coffee cart at the end of the pier. "I didn't even think about this earlier. Do you want coffee?"

"No. I mean, thank you, but I don't want coffee." Just as she said it, his eyes darkened. And, well, she felt a bit of a zip in her body, too. That kiss had inspired a whole lot of feelings she'd carefully locked away for the past few years. After never thinking about kisses or hugs or sex, right at the moment it was all she could think about.

Time seemed to slow down as she glanced at him again. Muscles defined his arms. His legs and feet were tanned and golden-brown. He looked healthy and vibrant and completely attractive.

And he'd been kissing her.

Before she could embarrass herself further, she quickly stepped down into the cabin of the boat, delighted to see a berth big enough to sleep two—that is, if you didn't mind really snuggling. A few small benches, cabinets with locks and wide drawers for storage.

When she stepped up, Tyler was radioing in their course and untying the lines from the dock. "Hey, Remy," he said the moment he saw her. "Come have a seat and keep me company."

Moments later the motor was on and he was guiding them out of the marina, through the channel and finally out into the Gulf. Around them, other small pleasure craft motored and glided through the greenish-blue waters. They passed a school of fish. A few jumped up in their boat's wake, making Remy smile.

"Ready?" Tyler asked.

"For what?"

"To hoist the sails." With no small amount of effort, he gripped the lines and raised one of the vibrant white sails, which caught a gust of wind and propelled the boat forward.

Remy gasped and gripped the beautiful teak framing her cushion tighter.

Tyler chuckled as he drew up another sail, then guided the boat farther out to sea. *Cynthia* seemed to come alive, dancing over the waves with ease.

Above them, seagulls screeched their encouragement, darting suspiciously close a time or two. Obviously they were looking for a midmorning snack. Spray fanned her face, the saltiness of it spurring her senses. Blinking back a few drops of salt water, Remy grinned. She was so glad she'd said yes.

From his position near the front of the boat, he glanced her way. "You doing okay?"

"Better than okay. I'm wonderful!" she called out, pushing her sunglasses back over her head. "Thank you so much for taking me."

He said nothing for a moment, just stared at her and smiled. At first Remy wondered if she should repeat herself. Maybe he hadn't heard her?

"You're welcome. It's my pleasure."

There went that jolt again. But this time she knew exactly why she was feeling it. Tyler Mann was incredibly sexy. Even if nothing more ever happened between them. Even if he never kissed her again, she'd always be grateful for this moment.

She was alive. She was alive and living and for once felt optimistic and hopeful about herself and her future. Maybe she was going to be okay after all.

Maybe Mark had been right when he'd warned her not to die with him. Maybe she had been right to finally have listened.

All she knew was that the day was gorgeously sunny and bright, the man beside her was her only companion for the next several hours and she felt gloriously free. Never again would she take any of those things for granted.

Chapter Eight

"I don't believe I've ever had champagne for lunch," Remy said once their server at the Silver Pelican popped the cork of the bottle with a flourish, then deftly filled two flutes.

"Then it's about time you did." Tyler gently clinked her flute before sipping his icy bubbly drink. "Who knows? Maybe this could become a habit."

"I sure hope not. I wouldn't get anything done."

"I imagine you still would. You just might also enjoy life a bit more." As he watched her lips press against the crystal rim, he felt a bit protective of her. Since they'd met, he'd seen a few different sides of Remy. In every one she was strong...and alone. Did she not have anyone close who simply cared that she was happy? He hoped there was someone like that in her life. If not, he was ready to sign up for the task.

But instead of smiling at his quip, two lines formed on her forehead. "I enjoy life, Tyler. I may not be sipping champagne every day, but I do all right."

"That was a poor choice of words. I'm sorry."

She blinked. "No, I...I overreacted. It's no big deal." Looking thoughtful, she opened her menu, which gave Tyler the perfect opportunity to study her a little more.

It wasn't hard to do.

Truth was, he couldn't keep his eyes off her. Of course, that summed up how he'd been feeling all day. Remy away from the office was an intriguing mixture of naïveté and assuredness. It was as if she'd concentrated so much on her work that she'd forgotten how to relax.

He couldn't wait to take her out again—to encourage her to smile.

Moments later, after the server took their order and discreetly refilled their glasses, Tyler reached for her hand. As she curved her fingers around his, he said, "I don't know if you realized it, but we have something to celebrate."

"And that is?"

"You did a great job sailing today."

Her cheeks flushed. "I hardly *sailed,* Tyler. What I did was stay out of your way."

"You helped a time or two. Remember those knots you made when we docked?"

She chuckled. "I hope you double-checked them. I'd hate for your brother to return to *Cynthia*'s slip just to find I'd inadvertently let the boat loose."

"If that happened, I'd take the blame."

"No, if it happens, I'll take the blame." Slowly pulling her hand from his, she said, "To tell you the truth, I've rarely felt like I did today—so free and at peace. I felt like I could do anything this afternoon. Like I could be anyone I wanted to be."

"Because you could."

Instead of acknowledging his comment, she continued. "Actually, the way I was today surprised me. I'm usually the person in control. And if I'm not, I have a really hard time with it."

"Maybe it was time you let someone else guide you."

When she looked skeptical, he chuckled. "Okay, maybe it's sailing that suits you."

"I've been on the water a lot and it's never happened before."

"There's something about the physical effort of keeping the sails flying that I never get over. It's like becoming one with the boat." Hearing his words, he shook his head in embarrassment. "Sorry, I sound ridiculous."

Her eyes soft, she murmured, "Not at all. At least, not to me."

Seeking to lighten the mood, Tyler quipped, "Well, no matter how I felt at 'one' with anything, I'm feeling pretty grateful that I got us back to the marina without incident. I can sail, but I've had my share of mishaps. Hell, I wouldn't have been surprised if I'd gotten us stranded on a sandbank."

"But you didn't."

"You're right. I didn't." Leaning back, Tyler forced himself to look around so she wouldn't get spooked with him gawking at her like a lovesick pup.

The Silver Pelican had been around for years. Part of its charm had been its study in contrasts. Fine silver, linen and crystal had kept company with exposed pipes, a scarred cement floor and a definitely sparse decorating style. In the past, eating at the restaurant had given him the feeling of eating a fancy dinner in the middle of a warehouse.

But over the past four months the decor had undergone an extreme makeover. Hard cement had been replaced with thick planked floors. The walls were a creamy slate-blue instead of gunmetal-gray. Gone were the few old fishing and yachting memorabilia tacked helter-skelter on the entrance's walls. Now a few choice black-and-white photos were displayed in buffed silver frames. The wait staff in their black slacks and crisp white shirts complemented the linen tablecloths. Even at lunch, white pillar candles lit the center of each table.

A slight clearing of her throat brought his attention back to Remy. After smoothing the pad of one finger over the rim of her flute, she said, "So...why did you move here, Tyler? Really?"

"I wanted to be close to Cindy." That was the truth. It was almost the whole truth.

"Are you two really close?"

"Yes. I guess I never really did tell you about my family. Well, the short version is that both my parents died suddenly in a car accident. For years it was just Cindy and me. She's my twin. Did I tell you that?"

Amusement played along her lips. "I had no idea. What was that like, growing up with a twin sister?"

"Great." He grinned. "Sometimes I wish I could tell you all kinds of stories about the two of us fighting or something—it seems that what most kids do. But if I said we've had our share of fights, it wouldn't be true. The truth is, we've always gotten along. When we were little, our house was *the* house for everyone to come play at. Mom never cared about messes or noise. Cindy and I would have friends over and play pirates or house or ghosts in the graveyard...whatever we could. Then, when everyone went home and it was just the two of us again, we'd keep right on playing. She loved Legos as much as I did. Together we'd spend whole evenings building towns."

"It sounds ideal. I'm jealous. My brother, Tim, is three years older than me. We got along, but were never especially close. We still aren't, not really."

"Having Cindy—it was great. It was like we had someone in our corner. Always. Looking back, I'd say

my parents, Cindy and I all got along unusually well."
Tyler glanced at Remy, wondering if he was ever going
to be capable of completely describing how good his
childhood had been. "We were our own unit. Like the
Four Musketeers or something."

"You were lucky."

"We were. But after Mom and Dad died, we both
took it hard. Each of us took a semester off from college to take care of the house and to sort through their
things."

"It's nice that you two had each other."

"I needed her, Remy. Losing my parents at twenty-one
was tough, though I guess it is at any age." Picking up
his glass, he swirled the champagne a bit, liking the way
the sparkling liquid caught the sun just right. "Anyway,
we put everything in order and tried to get our minds
around all we'd lost. A few months later Cindy found
Keith."

"And you didn't find anyone?"

"No." When she frowned, he tried to clarify what he
meant. "I mean, I did find what I wanted—it just wasn't
a person. See, I wasn't looking for another relationship. I
wanted something different. I started interning at a software company my senior year. As soon as I graduated,
I was hired on full-time. Later on, bigger companies
recruited me. I was successful, Remy. Really successful.
It made me happy, and that's what I clung to."

Hearing his words out loud, Tyler almost apologized.
It wasn't like him to be so candid...so unguarded.

But instead of finding fault, she murmured, "I know
what that's like—finding work." Remy looked away
from him, almost as if she was being transported back
to a darker place. "It helps."

"My career definitely helped me." For a moment

Tyler was tempted to turn the tables and ask about her loss. About her husband, Mark, about what dreams she regretted never fulfilling. About why she never went to her family for help.

But instinctively he knew she'd never respond to that much of an invasion of her privacy. So he kept the conversation firmly focused on himself...though he was realizing that he, too, wasn't very comfortable talking about losses.

"I was good at sales. And since I never really had anyone to go home to, I worked really hard. No schedule was too demanding. No trip too tricky to schedule."

"No weekend too inconvenient to work."

He smiled. Few people understood that. "Exactly."

"Even with all that work, I'm still surprised you never found anyone special."

"I wanted to, but now I think it's good I never did. Back then, in Houston, I wasn't ready for an emotional commitment. I just wanted to think about items I could see. Cars. Stuff." He looked at her quickly, not sure if he was making any sense at all.

When she nodded, he continued, ready to share feelings with her that he'd never shared with anyone. "The things I thought were important, money and material items...well, they're tough to base a relationship around. And the women who were also attracted to those things... Well, they were great people, but the stuff we had...it wasn't what I wanted to make a life around."

Their lunches came. Scallops on a bed of rice and greens, beautifully presented with wedges of lemon and grilled asparagus. Remy flashed a smile. "This looks almost too pretty to eat. But I'll try my best."

Picking up his own fork, Tyler wondered if he'd even notice if his food tasted like cardboard. The intensity of his feelings for her overshadowed everything else at the moment.

He just hoped that feeling would stay awhile.

IT WAS CLOSE TO FIVE O'CLOCK when Tyler pulled up to Remy's house. For a moment she considered asking him in, then thought better of it.

Tyler Mann had been too "everything" today. Too gorgeous. Too attentive. Too perfect. For hours at a time she'd forgotten she was a widow. Forgotten to be sad. Had forgotten to be anything but a woman in the company of an exceptional man.

She wasn't sure how Tyler had managed it, but he'd held her hand the whole way home, even shifting gears with her fingers linked in his. And, to Remy's dismay, holding hands with him had felt natural. Sweet.

At her door he trailed one hand down her arm, settling on her hip. Bent his head slightly and brushed his lips across hers. The feeling was whisper-soft. Gentle.

Different.

Little by little a dormant spiral of desire spun forward, encouraging a response. She leaned close, rested her hands on his shoulders. And held on. Lips opened and met. His tongue darted forward. To her surprise, she heard herself moan. Oh, it had been so long.

So very, very long since she'd been kissed like this... kissed as if their touch was just the beginning.

One kiss became three. Tentative moves intensified. Deepened. He kissed her so slowly, so perfectly, she would have imagined that the moment was just as special to him, too—if she hadn't known better.

Surely Tyler had been on dozens of dates like this. This was probably nothing special for him. She just happened to be the happy recipient of all that charm for the afternoon.

Finally he stepped back. "Thank you for today."

"No, thank you. It was wonderful. Everything was... Everything was great."

To her dismay, he grinned. "I liked that kiss, too."

And before she could clarify what she'd meant—that she'd been talking about the champagne, about the scallops, about *Cynthia,* about how great and exhilarating it had felt to be out on the water—he was already walking back to his Corvette and sliding behind the wheel.

She barely had time to wave goodbye before he zipped away. Leaving her alone.

Her keys and sunglasses seemed to clatter unusually loudly when she tossed them onto the front table. Her beach bag felt heavier than ever when she carried it to the laundry room and quickly tossed the towels in the waiting washing machine.

The kitchen looked just as sparkling and neat as it ever did. Only a single cereal bowl rested in the stainless steel dishwasher.

Before stepping on the white carpet, Remy was careful to take off her spiffy new shoes. It wouldn't do to accidentally stain the carpet.

Unwilling to sit in the empty room with only the television for company, Remy quickly walked into the luxurious bathroom that Mark had taken such care to design.

As water sprayed onto the intricately carved Italian tile lining the shower, more than ever Remy felt sure of one thing—she had never felt more at a loss as to what to do next.

Chapter Nine

Answering phones at Carnegie was certainly one of the layers of hell, Tyler decided. It had to lie right between burning in fires and climbing ladders nonstop.

Time spent at work certainly felt never-ending.

So did the coffee and lunch breaks. He was allotted one ten-minute coffee break and one thirty-minute lunch break per eight-hour shift. During each time, he raced out of his vanilla-colored cubicle, anxious for the slightest change in scenery.

However, that quest was always futile. There was only one place for Carnegie employees to visit besides the bathroom and the hot and humid smoking area outside— the break room.

Tyler wasn't a fan of the rather drab kitchenette. It reminded him of his first apartment. Actually, the room with its pale yellow walls, tan linoleum and stark white countertops was depressing. The refrigerator looked old enough to have belonged to his parents, and the three microwaves always looked as if they'd lost the battle with a bottle of Pine-Sol.

Plus, there never seemed to be anything good in the three snack and drink machines.

Or in his lunch.

Not that he could blame anyone else for his unappetizing lunches. He packed his own meals.

Which brought up a whole other source of irritation—the fact that he'd come full circle to packing stale sandwiches again. When was the last time he'd packed his lunch? Seventh grade?

He couldn't believe he'd ever taken his hour-long lunches at a variety of restaurants for granted in his past life. Obviously he'd been a fool.

Looking into his sack, Tyler pulled out a lopsided peanut butter sandwich and a bag of chips. Just as when he was thirteen, neither item looked appetizing.

Well, at least the process of wolfing down the sticky sandwich gave him the perfect excuse not to talk. Lately the break-room conversation hovered around the sale on diapers at the local convenience store, some gal's search for a new look in eye shadow, bloating and water retention…and the elusive "iron lady" Ms. Greer.

"I heard she was here all day Sunday," Kaitlyn said as she nibbled on her usual lunch—a carton of strawberry yogurt and an orange. "I kind of feel sorry for her. I mean, all she does is work."

"I don't feel sorry for her at all. I heard she's gotten exactly what she's always wanted," said the middle-aged woman with permed hair who sat across from Tyler. "Several people have told me that she's never wanted a family. That's why she's so difficult to deal with. All she does is put a hundred percent of her time and energy into Carnegie."

A brunette standing in front of the pop machine nodded. "This place is her family. Her second home." With a sniff, she added, "It's sad, really."

Kaitlyn wrinkled her nose in confusion. "I thought her husband died."

"He probably couldn't wait to get away from her, she's so tough," Permed Lady said. "I mean, have you ever seen her smile?"

Tyler had. Thinking again of the way she'd practically smiled nonstop aboard the *Cynthia,* he wished others could have seen her then.

Or maybe not. Here they were, talking as if Mark's death hadn't affected her any more than losing a set of keys. It made him sick. So sick he couldn't sit quietly anymore. "Don't you think you all are being pretty harsh?" he asked. "Give her a break. She's got a lot of responsibility here. Plus, it can't be easy, watching your spouse die." He knew better than anyone in the room that it hadn't been easy for her at all.

"I'd feel sorrier for her if she was ever just a little bit understanding," the gal who'd gotten a root beer commented as she paused on her way out the door. "She passed on my hourly raise last month, saying my production numbers were low. I don't think I can be too harsh."

Tyler chomped on the last of his sandwich so he wouldn't make a mistake and comment on any of that. If he said a word, a steady stream of four-letter-word-filled insults was sure to emerge.

As a few more employees filtered out of the room, Kaitlyn scooted a little closer and squeezed his forearm. "Don't mind Emma. She's always complaining about something. If it wasn't being skipped over for a raise, it would be her boyfriend or her mother or the fact that it's hot in Florida."

"I'll remember that."

Leaning even nearer, close enough that Tyler caught the faint scent of honeysuckle, she murmured, "I'll tell you a secret. Her production numbers really did suck. She's as slow as molasses on the phone."

"So raises really are possible?"

"You bet." With a little pleased smile, she added, "I've gotten two in the past seven months. Shawn Wagner even went so far as to call me a model of efficiency."

"Congratulations."

Kaitlyn giggled.

A chime rang overhead, signaling the end of the first shift's break. Kaitlyn paused on her way out. "Tyler, you know...we never get much time to talk. We ought to plan to do something sometime soon. Away from here."

His mouth conveniently full, Tyler nodded weakly when she waited for an answer. As soon as she turned away and left, he leaned back against the chair. Well, he had another ten minutes. Maybe if he was lucky, he could spend at least a portion of it alone. He needed to figure out how he could get out of this place, fast.

And what he should do about Kaitlyn. He felt a slight attraction to her, but his feelings for Remy were real. He knew he was falling hard for her. He wanted to be with her again, wanted to see her every night.

And that kiss—it was so sweet, so stirring. He thought about the way her hips had felt next to his. The way her body had pressed against his, so soft, so willing. It was as if she'd been waiting for him to come to Destin. Waiting for him to love her.

But he also wasn't a fool. There was a very good chance that Remy would never want what he did. And honestly, if she didn't, he didn't know if that would be okay.

He wanted a family.

So, therefore, for better or worse, he kept Kaitlyn's offer in the back of his mind. Just in case. He should tell her he wasn't interested, but a small part of him kind of was. Things were going really slowly with Remy. And while he was fine with that, she hadn't exactly pressed him for another date.

And though he had a heck of a crush on her, his goal of marriage and babies hadn't gone away. If Remy wasn't ultimately interested in such things, Tyler knew he'd be tempted to try things with Kaitlyn.

Surely there was nothing wrong with keeping her in the wings, was there?

The door swinging open scattered his thoughts. So did the person who appeared. Shawn.

"Hey," he said as soon as he sipped a good amount of pop. "I've got ten more minutes."

She smiled quizzically. "That's okay. I'm not here to monitor you, just to get some coffee. How are things going?"

"Fine."

"Glad to hear it." After pulling out a mug and filling it to the brim, she surprised him by taking Kaitlyn's vacant spot. "And...your weekend? How was it?"

"It was good, too. And yours?"

"Oh, about like you'd imagine with four kids—hectic. Though Eddie and I did manage to go to Bishop's Gate on Saturday night. We spent the night in his parents' condo and spent most of Sunday hanging out on the beach with the kids."

"My sister has two girls I try to see as much as I can. What are yours? Girls? Boys?"

"The grand total is three girls and one extremely active baby boy." Comically, she rolled her eyes. "I tell you, I thought after three kids nothing could surprise me, but he's sure giving me a run for my money. He's super active and always looking for trouble. He's hit every milestone earlier than any of the girls."

"Boys are more physical, I guess."

"Eddie says the same thing." After a moment's pause, she nonchalantly said, "So, what did you do?"

Her tone seemed a little too nonchalant. A weird sense of foreboding hit him hard in the solar plexus. "I went sailing."

"Ah. I thought it looked like you had some color on your cheeks." Stirring her coffee, she smiled. "Have a good time?"

"I did."

"I don't know if you heard…but Ramona went sailing, too."

"Ms. Greer did? Hmm." Tyler reached for his sandwich, then realized he'd finished it during the last uncomfortable conversation. "I hope she had a good time."

Shawn narrowed her eyes. "Did the two of you go together?"

Since he was the one who'd promised to keep their date private, he volleyed back a question. "Why would you ask that?"

"No reason. But…did you?"

Ten years of selling software had made him a pro at evading direct questions. "I'm sorry, but page twenty-seven of the handbook suggests I refrain from gossiping."

"Tyler, I think it's time you were honest with me. Is there something going on with you and Ramona?"

Every single bit of manly pride wanted to look her right back in the eye and say yes. It wasn't in his makeup to sneak around and pretend to be something he wasn't.

Though, to his dismay, he seemed to be doing a pretty good job of that lately.

Since Shawn was still waiting for a reply and he was tired of being fed questions, he went on the offensive. "Forgive me if I'm mistaken, but none of this seems work related. Or does answering your questions about my personal life fall into my job description? I'd hate to feel that I was being judged for that."

She blinked, obviously ill at ease. "No...I was just curious."

He almost smiled. There. Now she knew how it felt to be in the hot seat. Standing up, he pointed to the clock. "I really don't have anything to say about her. And, you know, I better get going. Don't want to be late. Around here, the clock is always ticking."

"Hold on." Lowering her voice, she said softly, "Tyler, I don't know if you know this, but Remy...Ramona's a good friend of mine."

"I'm glad."

"I'd hate to see her get hurt by someone just out for a good time."

Like Shawn, he wasn't born yesterday, either. "Duly noted. And just so you know, I don't discuss the women I date. Certainly not at work. Ever."

"That's good to know," she said slowly.

He opened the door just as the damn clock chimed. Not two minutes after he put on his headset, his phone lit up. "Thank you for calling Carnegie Airlines," he said as brightly as his sense of pride would allow.

"Sir, I wonder if you could help me. I'm trying to get to Miami...."

As Tyler wrote down the woman's requests and listened to her chat about her father, her four-year-old and the high price of cereal at her local grocery store, he gritted his teeth with impatience. He really hated this job.

Never again would he hang up on a telemarketer. Living on the phone all day sucked. It really did.

Chapter Ten

At ten to seven two days later, just minutes before the end of his shift, Tyler had the misfortune to answer a call from one of the most difficult men he'd talked to in his extremely short career at Carnegie.

After listening to a two-minute tirade about the guy's grievances, Tyler decided to calmly interrupt. Honestly, the guy needed a shrink, he was so delusional. "Sir, I'm not sure how Carnegie Airlines can help find your bags at the Orlando airport. That really sounds like a problem for the baggage handlers there."

"Well, no one here wants to get me my bag, so you better figure out how you can help," the caller—Mr. Ken Snyder—snapped. "Everyone in that cramped, dirty baggage claim office just keeps milling around, asking me to fill out a stinking form. I don't want to fill out a form. I want my suitcase."

"I'm sorry, but I'm unable to help you there."

"I don't want to hear that, you idiot. Tell me what you can do."

"Hold on, now. There's no need to call me names."

"There's every need. You should be offering me some kind of compensation," the caller shouted in Tyler's ear. "After all, it's your fault the bags are lost."

Tyler was getting pretty damn tired of being insulted

by strangers over the phone. Furthermore, he was getting pretty tired of dealing with nincompoops who constantly blamed him for things that weren't his fault.

Like this baggage mishap.

Who knew what might have happened to the guy's bags? Maybe the baggage handlers had stuck the bags on the wrong carousel. Maybe the suitcases had completely missed a connection. Shoot, maybe someone was having a coffee break instead of searching for luggage.

But it was not Tyler Mann's fault. He was just the poor schlep sitting in a confined space in Destin, Florida, for eight hours a day. All in the futile effort of getting a date.

He took a deep breath. Recalling Kaitlyn's warning to be nice and Shawn's warning about trying a little harder, Tyler asked, "Mr. Snyder, one more time, what did they say at the baggage office?"

"They seem to think it's not their fault that I missed my flight and decided to take a different connection." Mr. Snyder settled down a bit now, and his fury cooled to a whine. "Now we're sitting here in Orlando with nothing to wear. I need clothes, pronto. My kids are screaming. They want to see Mickey right now."

"I see."

"There was a blizzard in Buffalo, did you know that? The traffic was terrible. I couldn't help missing my scheduled flight."

"No, I, um, hadn't heard about the snowstorm." Tugging down his cuff, he saw that his shift was over. All he had to do was get the guy off the phone, and then he could be free.

"Why not? Don't you work for the airline?"

"I do. But I sit in an eight-by-eight cubicle all day. Plus I'm in Destin," he said nastily. "The weather's always great here. Now, as for your bags, I bet they'll show up within twenty-four hours."

"That's not good enough. Who do I talk with to get a check? We need to go shopping for clothes. ASAP."

Little irritated him more than people who threw around acronyms. "No one. It's not going to happen."

"Listen, you sack of—"

He'd had enough. "No, you listen. There's nothing I can do. Why don't you go relax or something? Go to Disney World. Your bags will get there as soon as they can."

"I. Want. The. Manager."

No way was he going to subject Shawn to this guy. Turning his voice sickeningly sweet, he replied, "I'm so sorry, but there's no manager around. I'm your only hope." Tyler couldn't help but grin. There. That ought to show the guy how to settle down.

"Actually, there's a manager right here," Remy Greer said just above his left shoulder. "And this manager would love to have the phone. Now."

Craning his neck to the side, Tyler turned her way… and then looked up. Up to the neat-as-a-pin navy suit. Up to the demure hint of cleavage under a yellow silk camisole. Up to her hair, pinned fussily on top of her head. Up to her lethal glare. "Crap."

"What?" screamed Mr. Snyder. "Are you swearing at me now?"

"Oh, settle down. Believe me, if I was swearing at you, you'd—"

Remy's eyes turned fiery. "Hand me the phone. Now."

Without a word, Tyler unsnapped the headset and slapped it into her hands. Remy expertly slipped it on over her ear, adjusted the microphone, then introduced herself to the jerk on the line. "This is Ramona Greer, the manager of this call center. I'm so sorry for any inconvenience you may have had." Glaring Tyler's way, she added, "The person you were speaking with is new."

When she motioned for him to give up his chair, Tyler readily complied. During the next few minutes he reluctantly stood in awe as she talked calmly and sweetly listened to the diatribe.

"Yes, sir. I'm sure it's been a very trying experience."

Tyler wanted to gag.

Narrowing her eyes, she said, "Yes, good help is hard to find. Now, how can I make things easier?"

Tyler figured what the guy really needed was a swift kick in the rear.

He couldn't believe what Ken Snyder got instead.

Five minutes later she was promising money would be wired to the hotel, his bags located as soon as humanly possible and then rushed to his hotel. Even if it meant someone was going to have to drive the bags to Orlando from Tampa.

Amazing.

When she hung up, he clapped, somewhat sarcastically. "That was impressive. I didn't know we could promise so much so quickly." He was joking, of course. There was no way anyone who worked for Carnegie was going to get paid to track down one rude little guy's bag.

"Actually, Tyler, I think you did. The correct procedures are listed very clearly in the handbook. And I believe Shawn spoke to you, as well."

"I can't believe you're getting so riled up."

"It's my job to help customers. To listen to their

needs." Narrowing her eyes, she added, "It's also yours."

"All right. Well, next time I'll try to be more patient."

"I'm sorry, but there won't be a next time."

"What?"

All of a sudden he was aware of most everyone in the vicinity listening in. Kaitlyn had even pushed her rolling chair out so she could watch him.

"You've left me no choice. Today's call now makes two irate customers you couldn't handle. And those are just the ones we know about. You are fired."

"What?" For a moment, she'd sounded as if she'd just come off Donald Trump's show.

"I'm sure you heard me."

"Oh, I heard you, all right, but I don't understand."

With a huff, she unhooked his phone, slipped off his headset, then stood up next to him, glaring at him with enough frost that ice would probably start forming any moment. "Come. With. Me."

Next door, two call representatives moaned.

Tyler rolled his eyes Kaitlyn's way, then grabbed his cell phone and lunch sack and quickly followed Remy out of the maze of cubicles.

She didn't say a word as she strode down the aisles. He traded embarrassed glances with a few people who looked up in alarm.

Up the stairs they went. Tyler couldn't help but notice how pretty she looked in navy patent leather heels.

Past Shawn's desk they strode. Into Remy's office. As soon as he stepped in, Remy shut the door behind her with a decisive click.

Then she breathed deeply, obviously striving for control.

God, she looked hot.

He tried to joke. "I really am sorry about that guy. But nothing he was saying made sense, Remy. You've got to know that. He was an SOB."

Shaking her head weakly, she murmured, "Tyler, this was a mistake."

She'd lost him. "What was?"

She waved a hand around the room. "Everything. For ever thinking you would like working here." Picking up a bottle of Perrier, she continued, "This was a mistake, too."

He wasn't following her. "The water?"

"No. I mean you. I mean *you* were the mistake." Her eyes narrowed. "You really were."

"Don't you think you're getting a little carried away?"

"Not at all."

Now he was getting irritated. "I must have taken thirty calls today. You had the misfortune of hearing the bad one. I did fine with everyone else."

"That's the problem. That's what you're not understanding. See, there can't be *any* bad calls. We can't only try to please some people some of the time. When people call here, we need to try for a hundred percent customer satisfaction."

"But not everyone can be satisfied."

"But we have to try." Shaking her head, she stared at the green glass bottle in her hand. "Tyler, the fact is, I shouldn't have hired you. I'm sorry I ever did."

He stood closer, tried to reach for her hand. She pulled it away as if his touch burned. "Stop."

"Stop what? I may be your employee, but I'm still the same person I was last weekend. I'm the guy you went sailing with, remember? You had no problem holding my hand then."

"That was a mistake. I shouldn't have gone. I shouldn't have dated an employee."

Why was she making everything so hard? Why was she overanalyzing everything between them? The solution to their problems was staring her in the face. "Remy, don't you see? Everything is all good now. Since you're firing me, I won't be working for you anymore. Now we have no problem."

Remy closed her eyes and looked as if she was trying hard to count to ten. She must have failed, because seconds later she was glowering. "Yes, we do. And if you can't see that, then I'm afraid we're done."

"So you're firing me and dumping me over one idiot from Buffalo?"

"If that's how you see it...yes."

"I don't. But it's a shame that's how you do."

"Please collect your things and leave."

Lifting his cell, he almost smiled. "This is the only thing I need to collect, Remy. I think I'll just take my sorry self out of here right now. I'm sure you have my paperwork on file. My address is there, too. You can just mail me anything you need me to sign."

She folded her arms across her chest. "You know this isn't my fault."

"Oh, yes it is, Remy. So far you haven't listened to a thing I've said. Not about the idiot. Not about our date. Not about us. And worse, you haven't been listening to the things you've said to me, either." He turned to her before throwing open her office door. "You should have listened, Remy. You should have believed in me. In us. Because, see...I was so worth your time."

"Goodbye, Tyler."

"Bye." Without looking back, he strode out. Passed Shawn and strode down the stairs. Passed a few people standing outside the break room, obviously hoping to catch a little bit of fresh office gossip.

He couldn't get out of the building fast enough.

Remy had been right about one thing. Working at Carnegie call center had been a mistake. Phenomenal.

So had basing a relationship on a well-written magazine article and a pair of sad gray eyes.

So had imagining that a few kisses and meaningful looks meant anything more than what they were. It had all been a mistake. A big one. And now he was paying the price.

Chapter Eleven

"You don't look so good, Señora Greer," Carmen said when Remy walked in the back door that evening. "Bad day at work?"

"It was one of the worst. One of the top ten worst ever."

Carmen shook her head. "Those customers should remember that you cannot be more than you are. You cannot help it if the rain and snow cancel flights." Folding her arms across her chest, she added, "Or if flight attendants are rude."

Looking at her housekeeper with real fondness, Remy said, "You're better than a therapist, Carmen. You always tell me exactly what I need to hear."

"Did it help?"

"Not today, I'm afraid. Unfortunately, today's problems were all my fault. I had to fire someone this afternoon. It was the guy I went out with last weekend. The guy who took me sailing."

Carmen's eyes brightened with speculation as she sat down at the kitchen table. "Señora Greer, I sure can't be thinking about dusting the living room now. You'll have to tell me everything. This news you have is too bad."

It *was* too bad. At the moment her whole life felt that way. Slowly, without elaborating too much, she told

Carmen all about their sailing trip, and the phone call she witnessed.

"He's just not cut out for the job. People think it's easy, but it's not. It can be really challenging. Heck, I know some of the people who call in are difficult."

"That's putting it nicely, yes?" Pulling over the fruit bowl, Carmen picked up an orange, rolled it between her palms, then started peeling it.

"Well, yes. But the things we deal with aren't a surprise, either. Everyone who's hired knows what he or she is getting into."

"Ah, yes. You've talked about that before." Smiling slightly, Carmen carefully placed another chunk of peel in the neat pile in front of her. "Everything about Carnegie is all in your handbook."

Was Carmen being sarcastic?

"That's right," Remy answered, deciding after a moment not to read anything into Carmen's words. "He should have read the handbook more carefully. And listened to Shawn's advice, too."

"But he didn't."

"Nope. Tyler's too opinionated, too strong to be yelled at about unreasonable requests. I knew that when I hired him." Remy slumped against the back of her chair, kicking off her heels in the process. "I knew it as soon as he introduced himself."

When Carmen glanced her way, Remy added, "But, oh, he had the best handshake."

"Humph. And he was handsome, no?"

"He was. I mean he is. He's so handsome. He's so everything." Closing her eyes for a moment, Remy muttered, "He always smells good, too."

"And now he's gone."

It sounded so final. "Yep, Carmen. Tyler's so gone

from my life. He's so gone, and I'm the one who pushed him out of it, too."

Carmen pulled off a succulent slice of orange and popped it into her mouth. "Oh, Señora Greer, don't worry so. Something will happen. Maybe."

"Maybe. Maybe doubtfully." Though she'd known she had no choice but to fire him—there was no way she could have saved face with everyone if she'd let him get away with that attitude—she still knew come Monday, she was really going to miss him.

Miss that voice. "Did I tell you that he's from Houston? He's got the best accent. It's kind of low and there's this gravelly drawl, too. It's awesome." She practically got chills up and down her spine every time she thought about it.

Never mind his kisses.

Carmen fanned her face before popping another slice into her mouth. *"¡Dios mio!"*

"I know! Now I won't ever see him again."

"Señora Greer, are you upset that you had to fire this man or because you won't see him no more?"

Remy lifted one eyebrow. "Are we being honest?"

"Always."

"Both. Well, okay, mainly that I won't see him anymore. Which is stupid, because I told him going out together had been a mistake."

"Because?"

"Because he scared me. He made me feel alive again."

"Señora Greer, maybe that's how you should feel, *sí?*"

Remy couldn't answer. She was afraid to.

Carmen stood, deposited the orange peels in the trash, then bustled around the kitchen, her soft-soled shoes squeaking as they always did. Remy watched her neatly fold a dish towel and slide it into the drawer to the left of the sink, then, seemingly satisfied that everything was as it should be, she went to the hall closet and picked up her purse. "I think I'll go home now."

Feeling slightly let down, Remy nodded. "Oh. Okay."

Looking as stern as Remy had ever seen her, Carmen said, "Señora Greer, I have something more to say. You should...you should call him."

"I can't."

"You should."

Remy could only imagine how that would go over. "And say what? That I'm sorry I fired him?"

"No, no, no. Señora Greer, you need to take the job out of your mind."

"I can't—"

Carmen interrupted. "I think you've forgotten that your life didn't used to be all about work. It used to be about having fun, too. Maybe it's time you remembered that?" She paused at the door. "Don't forget that I won't be here the rest of the week."

"You're going to Tampa, aren't you?"

"Oh, yes. My newest grandson is getting christened. All my family will be there."

"I hope you have a good time. Hug everyone for me."

"I will." Wagging a finger, Carmen glared at her again before opening the back door. "Remember what I said, Señora Greer. There's more to life than work. And more to you, too. I promise."

Still seated at the kitchen table, Remy listened to Carmen start her car and drive off. Carmen was right about there being more to her than just work.

She knew that, too. And she did have other friends. And Mark's family was wonderful. Yes, there were lots of people she could do things with. Of course, they were longtime friends…friends who'd been at her wedding and had stayed by her side during Mark's illness. Later they'd been incredibly supportive during the weeks after his funeral.

And they still asked her to do things. As a matter of fact, she'd been invited to a party on the weekend. She just hadn't planned to attend.

But maybe she should consider going. And the next time someone introduced her to a man, perhaps she should actually smile and flirt a bit.

Perhaps if she'd been a little more outgoing, she wouldn't have been so hung up on Tyler. She'd feel a bit more like she used to feel.

Who knows? Maybe a conversation could lead to a phone call or a date? Maybe then she'd have a reason to put on something besides a suit.

She missed feeling feminine. To have a reason to buy strappy sandals and a dress that showed a bit too much cleavage. To buy a black lace nightgown—one that wasn't very comfortable or warm—because she never planned to sleep in it.

At forty-two, it seemed kind of sad all that was in her past.

Of course, it didn't have to be. Just recently she'd gone sailing. She'd been with someone who didn't expect her to be a martyr. Who didn't whisper that she was a widow.

Who kissed her as if she wasn't too old to have romance in her life.

It was just too bad that he was the wrong guy. So wrong…in every way possible.

* * *

TO TYLER'S DISMAY, Cindy burst out laughing when he told her he'd been fired.

"How long did that job of yours last? Ten days?"

"I was there four weeks." It had seemed longer, though.

Still giggling, his sister tucked her tanned legs up on the couch after she poured them each a glass of crisp chardonnay. "Ty, you actually sound upset! We both know this so wasn't the job for you. A call-center cubicle would be the last place on earth where you would be happy. What are you going to do now?"

He sipped his wine, appreciating its icy tartness as they sat on her back deck and watched the sun glide low, then seem to sit suspended over the horizon. "Sit here with you."

"And then?"

"I don't know."

"Ty, you're not going to leave me, are you?"

He heard the edge in her voice and felt her agitation. The worry. "No way. Cindy, I meant it when I promised I'm going to live close to you. To stay that way."

"But if the job situation—"

"Is no big deal," he finished. "I'll find something here. I will. I want to see the girls. I want us to be close again." Those promises, at least, were not difficult to keep.

"I want us to stay close, too." Below them, a pair of teens walked on the winding path toward the beach. After just a few steps the boy pulled the long-legged girl into his arms and kissed her.

Cindy watched them and smiled. "Oh, look at them. They're so cute, so in love. Remember feeling like that, Ty?"

"Being horny? Yeah."

She picked up one of the crackers she'd been nibbling and tossed it at him. "Shut up. I'm talking about young love. Of not being able to wait another minute before sneaking another kiss. All that anticipation. That's how I was with Jeremy."

He turned away from the teens, who were now rolling around in the sand, and looked at his sister in surprise. "Well, there's a name I haven't heard in a while."

"I may not talk about him…but I sure haven't forgotten the guy. Jeremy was a big part of my life, you know. He was special."

Jeremy had been her high school boyfriend. Cindy would never guess, but Tyler knew for certain that Jeremy's yearnings had never been especially chaste or sweet.

To Tyler's disgust, Jeremy had never been shy about telling everyone on the team about his feelings for Cindy Mann. Tyler had had to pound the kid once for talking trash about his sister. "I'm glad you broke up with him."

"Oh, stop. All I'm saying is that sometimes I miss those feelings. Of course I love Keith, but we're married and have kids and sometimes only talk about feedings and nap time and schedules." She sighed. "It's been a while since we've been all hot and bothered."

Tyler supposed he'd miss feeling that way, too…if he hadn't been feeling extremely hot and bothered the past few weeks.

Choosing Cindy's euphemism, he knew he'd been all full of "young love," too. Now, even though Remy had tossed him out of the office, he still wanted to take her out to dinner. To watch her emotions run through her eyes. "You ever hear what happened to old Jeremy?"

"Yeah," she replied, her tone flat. "Last I heard, he got some navy groupie pregnant when he was on leave. Now they're living on a base in California."

This time it was Tyler who couldn't help but laugh. "I guess he was still searching for some of that 'young love,' too."

Cindy responded by pouring them another glass of wine. "Let Jeremy be a lesson to you, brother. Sometimes those yearnings don't last. You need to concentrate on common likes and interests. Stability. Chances are what you felt for Remy probably wasn't the real thing."

"It felt real."

Raising her glass, she shrugged. "Perhaps. But I'd bet a dollar that this older woman was probably not the one for you. It's probably a blessing that she fired and broke up with you all at the same time. Try looking for someone a little more fun, Ty. Someone more like you."

Thinking about how easy Remy was to be around, about how much he'd enjoyed sailing with her, he said, "She is."

"Maybe, though I don't think so. If she'd been so perfect, you would've been eager for her to meet us."

"No, I wouldn't have. We only went sailing, Cindy. And just because she broke up with me, I haven't given up hope."

"Well, promise me this. If you two see each other again, why don't you let us meet her?"

"Leave it, Cindy." Feeling frustrated, with both himself and with how poorly things were going, Tyler sipped his wine and watched the sun continue to set.

The bright orange ball now hung so low, it illuminated the sea. Within minutes it would be dark and the cranes would come out circling for the next meal.

Yes, life always went on. No matter what happened, life would go on. Even if your parents died, hours continued to pass. Even if a spouse was diagnosed with cancer. Even if you lost a job.

By his side, Cindy nibbled her lip, looking obviously frustrated. "I'm sorry if I said too much, Ty. If I pushed too hard. It's just…I care. That's all."

"I care about you, too. Don't worry. Everything will work out. If I never see Remy again, I'm sure I'll meet someone new. And if a miracle happens and Remy and I start dating again, I'll let you meet her. I promise."

Trust and happiness sparkled in her eyes. "That's all I need to hear. Thank you." Finally they settled into a companionable silence, happy to just sit and listen to the waves crash against a formation of rocks below. Tyler forced himself not to wish for anything more.

Chapter Twelve

The dinner party had been brutal. Oh, the company had been fine, but Remy had never felt more alone or single. The only bright spot was that Craig and Janice had been invited, too. Remy and Mark used to join them for dinner every once in a while. Back when he'd been healthy.

So the night had started off well enough. But then she'd discovered that Craig and Janice had planned a little surprise with the hostess.

They'd brought along Blake—Remy's prospective date. When she'd learned that news, it had been all she could do to keep a smile on her face. Every bit of her had been screaming for her to run for cover. Yes, she'd hoped to meet someone, but not like this. Not a meeting where the guy looked as if he'd been pushed her way, like a sacrificial lamb.

Not that Blake was horrible. He hadn't been at all. In fact, Blake had been nice. He was attractive in that fifty-year-old way, too. He'd somehow managed to become successful in the banking industry and, wonder of wonders, was doing well.

Actually, everything about him—from his haircut to his Italian-cut suit—screamed success and money and class. He was confident and pleasant and extremely well mannered.

In addition, there was a glint in his eyes signaling that he found her attractive. "Ramona, I can't believe we've never run into each other before."

"I don't date much."

His eyes clouded. "I've been through tough times, too. Margaret, my wife, left me eighteen months ago. Said she was tired of being married."

"I'm sorry."

He shrugged. "Thanks, but I think I'm over the worst of it. And I'm better off without her. She had an affair."

Though a small part of her was rebelling from hearing about his troubles only moments after meeting him, the greater, more mature part of her figured it took a pretty special type of guy to admit such secrets. "That had to be tough."

"It was. Counseling helped. And…life goes on, you know."

"You're exactly right." Life did go on. She'd sure been hearing that a lot lately. It would be a good thing to remember. And, once more, she should be happy that such a guy was interested in her. She should be flattered to have his attention. She should be enjoying his company.

"So, maybe we could see each other again?"

She gritted her teeth. Remembering the promise to herself, she forced herself to smile. "I'd like that."

Blake smiled, then excused himself—a buddy of his was signaling for him. For a moment Remy stood there, a little taken aback by his hasty exit. Then, to her amazement, she noticed he was speaking to yet another woman. One who wasn't wearing a wedding ring, either.

Had she just been taken in by a few great lines?

Ugh. Just the thought of that left a bad taste in her mouth.

Later, when he circled back and asked for her number, she conveniently forgot to give it to him, though Blake would most likely just get it from one of her friends.

Emotionally exhausted, she left the party soon after.

Remy had been uncomfortable the whole time. Blake—or anyone just like him—wasn't who she wanted to be with. No, that person was taller, younger and far more handsome. And he didn't drive a Mercedes. He drove a Corvette.

Throwing her keys onto the little tray on the table in the front hallway, Remy stood for a long moment. Gazed around the empty foyer. Around the professionally decorated living room.

Automatically she started walking to the guest bedroom. A conversation with Mark always made her feel better. But now, for some reason, the thought of an imagined conversation with a man who would never hold her again made her feel even worse.

No, she wanted someone real. Someone made of flesh and blood. Someone who made her feel right. Turning around, she knew there was only one option. And she had to do it or she was going to go crazy.

Crossing the foyer to her office, she pulled out her briefcase and snatched up a small white sheet of paper she'd scribbled a number on. Tyler's phone number.

She glanced at the clock—nine-thirty. And, as luck would have it, it was Saturday night. There was no way he was going to be home. Loss suffused her. Resolutely she knocked it away. Though Blake had been incredibly full of himself, he had made a good point. Life did go on—and it was for the living.

Now she needed to take a first step. All she had to do was gather her courage, dial Tyler's number and then leave him a message—surely he would be too busy to be answering his phone so late at night.

But tell him what? She wasn't sorry she'd fired him. He really had been horrible at his job.

Wincing, she could almost hear Carmen's advice flow through the halls. *There is more to life than work.*

No, all she had to tell Tyler was...the truth. She simply needed to admit that she, too, had thought there was something special between the two of them. That she, too, had liked going sailing. That she'd liked being with him.

And that she missed him.

And even though their work relationship was over, she didn't want their personal relationship to be. Heck, they were both mature adults who could overcome personal differences.

Yeah!

Besides, it wasn't as if he'd loved working at Carnegie. He could find other jobs, jobs far more suited to his skills and capabilities than he'd ever find at the call center.

Yes. That sounded smart. Assured. Confident. Like a woman who knew what she was doing with her life. Who wasn't frozen in the past and holding tightly to the things that used to be.

The worst thing that could happen was that he would never call her back.

No, the worst thing that could happen would be if she never took a chance. If she never called him and just sat around going to dinner parties and being set up with bank executives.

She picked up the phone. Still standing, she punched

in his number. Counted the rings. Waited for his voice mail to click on.

Nearly dropped the phone when she heard his voice.

"Hello? Remy, is that you?"

Shoot! "I'm sorry," she blurted. "I mean, yes. Hi. I...I didn't think you'd answer the phone."

To her relief, he sounded amused instead of put off. "Let me get this straight. You're sorry I answered when you called me?"

Why don't you just try to insult him a bit more? she told herself. *If you try harder, you could even manage to put him down while you're at it!* "No," she said quickly. "I spoke without thinking. I didn't mean that."

"You spoke without thinking, Remy? I find that hard to believe." His voice was rolling with a mixture of sarcasm and gentle teasing. Warmth, too.

"I guess I deserved that." When he didn't reply, she shuffled the phone against her shoulder and weighed her options. She could either move forward and be tough... or continue to live her lies. "I would say I don't know why I called, but I do. I'm just going to say this. I...I liked our date."

"I did, too."

"And while you might find it hard to believe, I never associated our date...our relationship with work."

"How *did* you think about us, Remy?"

She thought of them, together, as scary. The way she felt around Tyler made her uncomfortable. Unnerved. Almost bad—because when she was with him she felt pretty and sexy and alive. As if most of her hadn't died with Mark.

But that wasn't the right thing to say. It was too honest. "I had a nice time. I enjoyed being with you." As soon as the words left her mouth, she closed her eyes. What. Was. She. Doing?

"So, was there a reason you called? You know, besides hoping I wouldn't answer?"

Ooh, his voice was like warm syrup, coating her insides. Making her feel all warm and perfect. "I didn't call for anything specific. I mean, I guess you were on my mind."

"Because?"

"I was set up at a party. The guy—he was exactly my type. But it didn't feel like it. Because…because I had more fun with you." Oh, it was *so* time to get off the phone. "Never mind. Listen, I think I'll just—"

"Are you home now?"

"Yes." *Why does he care?*

"I mean—will you be home for a while? Will you be home for the night?"

"Yes." Doubts set in again. Darn it, she'd probably answered too quickly. She shouldn't have sounded so eager. She shouldn't have tried to make a date.

"Listen, I'm actually not at home. I'm at my sister's."

"Oh. I'm sorry." Now she was completely embarrassed. His whole family would know he had a stalker!

"What I meant was, I'm pretty close to you. I'll be there in twenty minutes."

He was on his way over? Her pulse quickened. "You sure?"

"I've never been more sure. And, Ramona?"

"Yes?"

"Look for me, would you?"

He hung up before she could ask him what, exactly, he

meant, though she knew. It was time to grow up. Time to move on, for better or worse.

Glancing in the mirror, she gasped. She was still wearing her black cocktail dress. She looked severe and boring. So not what she wanted to greet him wearing. And now she had less than twenty minutes to put on something pretty. In a flash she ran to her closet. After a moment's doubt she pulled out a pair of ivory knit pants and a matching zip-up. It was casual but formfitting. Definitely not staid.

A quick glance in the mirror led her to pull off her chunky gold earrings, unpin her hair and dab on some sheer pink lip gloss.

Next she trotted to the kitchen and pulled out two wineglasses. Wondering if she should make a cheese and cracker tray, she opened the refrigerator and stared inside...then called herself a fool.

What she needed to do was relax and be herself.

She just hoped she'd remember who that was before Tyler pulled up in her drive.

"I DON'T THINK YOU SHOULD go over there," Cindy warned, pure steel in her voice. "This is nothing but a booty call."

Tyler almost dropped the shirt he'd loosely been holding while tossing an extra shirt, socks, boxers and a few condoms into the gym bag lying open on his bathroom counter. Once again, he'd elected to stay at Cindy's house for the weekend instead of his empty apartment. "I swear, every time I think you can't surprise me, you do. Where'd you learn that term? You're married. With children!"

"I read *Cosmo*. I watch TV."

"I think guys are the ones who make the booty calls, Cindy."

"Not in this day and age. You should have seen some of the cougars on *Lipstick Jungle*—those women would have their claws in you in no time flat."

It really was kind of cute that his sister was so protective. Especially when she conveniently forgot that they were the same age.

Especially since at the moment he would be perfectly fine with a "booty call." He'd wanted Ramona Greer from the first moment he'd seen her. "I better get going. I told her I'd be there in twenty minutes."

"Jeez! She can't even wait? Her behavior is bordering on embarrassing. Just because you're handsome doesn't mean you're easy."

"Bye, Cindy."

Pointing to his gym bag, she glared. "I think it's a mistake to take all those clothes over there."

"I'm going to leave my bag in the car. I just want to be ready in case something does happen."

"Humph." Crossing her arms, she murmured, "What about breakfast? Megan was planning on it."

"I'll call you early and let you know. But I wouldn't count on me coming back here tonight, Cin."

"Because you're going to sleep with her."

Though four packs of condoms were staring right back at him, he shook his head. "I don't know what we're doing. I don't think sex is what she has in mind," he added. "I think she just wants to talk."

"But if she does only want one thing, don't you think that's a little creepy?"

On impulse, he threw in a pair of swim trunks, too. Who knew what they'd be doing? "Cindy, do you really want me to get involved in your life? You know, start giving you warnings about Keith? How if you're not careful he could break your heart?"

"That's pretty much an impossibility. Besides, it's a little too late for a bunch of warnings," she said dryly.

"It's too late for me, too. I know what I'm doing."

"I just don't want her to break your heart."

"Kiss those girls for me." After kissing her forehead, he walked out her front door and tossed his bag into the passenger side of the Corvette. Just as he opened the driver's door, he was amused to see Cindy still standing in her doorway, looking glum. "Wish me luck."

She waved a hand. "You won't need luck. Not tonight, anyway. Be careful driving."

"Thanks, sis. Bye."

Ten minutes later he announced his name to the guard at the gated community, then parked in Remy's driveway.

Don't mess this up, he cautioned himself. *Don't push too hard. Let Remy set the tone.*

With a bit of trepidation, he got out of the car. Clicked the lock. Then the front door opened.

And while Remy definitely wasn't running toward him like a reunion in an old movie, she did walk down the front steps to meet him. "You came."

"I did." As he followed her inside, he noticed quite a few things about her.

She was smiling, her eyes pretty. A cloud of something expensive floated around her. So different from the girls who seemed to all wear one of the many trendy fragrances that smelled like soap.

No, she smelled delicate and feminine and gorgeous. Almost as pretty as she looked. Without looking behind him, he nudged the door shut.

The white marble floor matched the silky white outfit

she was wearing. The top was zippered and trimmed in satin. The pants were flowy and had an elastic waist.

Her feet, previously seen only in high heels or sporty deck shoes…were bare.

Her toenails had little white lines at the end of each one.

She looked like a dream. Like his own personal, middle-of-the-night, don't-wake-him-until-he-embarrassed-himself dream.

"I chilled some wineglasses. Or I have club soda? Or a beer…"

"Anything's good." Anything that was wet, because his mouth had just gone dry. Just as she turned away, he'd caught sight of her firm little rear all covered in formfitting ivory fabric.

Peering into the fridge, she bent a bit. "I have water and juice, too."

"I don't care."

She turned to face him, her lips slightly parted.

That was when Tyler gave up all pretense of wanting to listen. Of pretending to only want to talk. "Hold…" he whispered. At the moment, he felt incapable of saying more than one word at a time.

"What?"

"This." After taking a step forward, he wrapped his arms around her and kissed her. Softly nibbling. Softly gliding his tongue against her parted lips. Coaxing them open. Tasting her.

She moaned. He responded by deepening the kiss. By holding her closer. Every sense ignited. He felt the tension in her shoulders, the soft curve of her rear. He felt her breasts flatten against his chest, and tasted mint and the faint crispness of cold wine.

She was intoxicating.

He nudged her feet apart and stepped closer. Cupped that rear. Glided his hands along her hips, enjoying how amazing her body felt encased in the clingy knit outfit.

She broke away slowly. Confusion swam in her eyes as she searched his face. "Tyler, I don't know what you thought. I didn't call you up for this."

"I know."

"But it's why you came over?" Hurt and confusion and embarrassment clouded those eyes. He knew the feelings. Shoot, he'd been fighting some of the same things himself.

"No. I wanted to see you. That's why I came over." Daring to smile, he leaned forward and nipped at the underside of her jaw. "But I'd be lying if I said I didn't want this, too. I've been dying to kiss you again. To touch you."

"Touch," she repeated, her voice all soft and husky. Then, with a shake of her head, she dropped her hands from his waist. Stepped back. "Listen. I still think we should talk. I mean, there's a lot we've got to talk about."

There was a reason he'd been so good in sales. He knew when to push…and when to back off. Immediately dropping his hands, he complied with her request. "I'll follow you, Remy. Lead the way."

With another doubtful smile, she walked across the kitchen, but there was a new sultriness in her walk. Her hips looked more fluid, her stride a bit more sexy.

Making him wonder if maybe she wasn't as unaffected by his kisses as she was trying to pretend to be. Though, to be honest, she really hadn't pretended to be unaffected at all, had she?

No, it was more as if she didn't trust her own emotions. Her own responses to him. That was interesting.

As for him, it was time he kept his mouth shut. Otherwise he was going to kiss her again. Or tell her she looked beautiful. Or say something stupid—like what, exactly, did she have on under that sweet little white outfit?

Chapter Thirteen

Oh, for heaven's sake. He thought she'd called him up to make love! To hook up—or whatever twentysomethings called it now.

But she hadn't called for that reason…had she? A dull, sick thought pooled in her stomach. Had she secretly been hoping that they'd end up in her bed? That by merely giving in to all the sexual chemistry between them, all their differences would magically disappear and not matter anymore?

Surely she was more together than that.

Still standing across from him, still reeling from the way her whole body had responded to his kisses, she attempted to cool things off.

Well, cool herself off. Motioning to the two wineglasses she'd set out, she murmured, "I don't think we ever settled the drink question. Do you like wine?"

His dimple appeared. "I like it just fine. Pour us some, Remy."

She glanced at him, trying to gauge his expression. "I've never met a man as easy to please as you."

"It depends on who's pleasing me."

Her hand shook as she poured wine. The golden liquid sloshed against the inside of the crystal before settling.

"I don't know what to make of you when you speak like that."

Tyler took one of the glasses from the counter before she could offer, then led the way to her living room.

She followed him across the white marble floor, again feeling out of sorts in his company. He did that to her. He let her take the lead, all the while never letting her forget that he was completely in charge of the situation.

It was a talent, that's what it was. A talent and a distraction, all at the same time.

Again she questioned herself. Why had she called him? No matter what happened, it always seemed as if he turned the tables and took charge. She couldn't recall things ever being that way with Mark. No, with Mark, things were more even.

How funny that she felt so vulnerable when she was the one who had so much going for her.

Perching on the edge of the cream couch, she went on the offensive. "So I was thinking that when things settle down, maybe we could see each other again."

"When do you want to do that?" In direct contrast to her tense perch on the couch, Tyler was leaning back, one ankle propped on the opposite knee. Looking as if he hung out there all the time. "When I've recovered from the loss of my job?"

"Put like that, I know it sounds pretty harsh."

To her surprise, he simply smiled. "I had my own reasons for taking that job, Ramona. Career advancement wasn't one of them."

"Care to tell me what your reasons were?"

"No." In one smooth movement he set down his glass and scooted closer to her. Close enough for her to smell his cologne. To realize that he'd shaved.

He watched her watch him with a bit of amusement. "Tell me about you and Mark."

That was completely unexpected. Placing her glass next to his, she murmured, "What do you want to know?"

"Whatever you want to tell me. Did you two have a good marriage?"

"Yes." She didn't know what else to say. Things with Mark had been good. She'd been happy with him, and knew that they would have had a great marriage for decades.

He waited a beat. "What did you do for fun?"

Fun? That took a moment to think about. They hadn't had much fun at all when he was sick. "Um. Well. We planned things," she said slowly. "We made plans. Mark loved to design and arrange."

"And you did, too?"

Did she? She couldn't really recall. "I liked being with him." She sidestepped his question. "His plans made me smile." Remembering a few incidents that she'd long ago pushed to the back of her mind, she chuckled. "And laugh. Oh, Tyler, you should have seen him with this house. Some people get so stressed building a house. Not Mark. He was in his element. Every day he'd run over here after work and putter around, looking and observing and asking a hundred questions."

"You did all that, too?"

"No." With some surprise, she said, "Actually, I hardly made any decisions about this place."

"Why not?"

She waved a hand around the room, with the built-in bookshelves and the amazing picture windows and the curious electronic gadgets she still managed to mess up. "I didn't care about it like Mark did. Truthfully, I didn't really need all this space. All these luxuries. I never asked for it. I just wanted a home."

Something flickered in his eyes, a new understanding. "I had a really nice home in Houston. I bought the place with my first really big bonus check. It was in a nice part of town. In Memorial. Pine trees covered the grounds. It was seven thousand square feet, had a four-car garage and a built-in sauna."

"It must have been really something."

"It was. I sold it to the first bidder and never looked back."

"Now where do you live?"

Looking amused, he said, "In a two-bedroom condo in Bishop's Gate. It's eight years old. Looks older. One of the bedrooms is painted a horrible shade of green. I haven't gotten around to painting it something better."

Bishop's Gate was a nice resort community, but definitely not known for being especially prestigious or fancy. "That's a nice area. It's pretty. Close to the beach."

"It is." He shrugged. "It's a place to be." Leaning to his side, he brushed his shoulder with hers. Right before he tilted his chin down next to her ear. "Remy, I don't want to compete with your husband. With Mark."

His words gave her chills. Or maybe it was the way his warm breath tickled her neck. "You don't."

"You sure?" He almost smiled. "Sometimes I feel like he's in the room with us, and I know I'll never completely have your attention." Reaching out, he gently fingered the tiny silver zipper pull on her top. Just played with it, not tugging at all.

But still her body responded. Her mouth went dry. Her nipples hardened. She hoped he didn't notice.

"Remy," he murmured, "I'm not trying to be the

man Mark was. To be the man you've saved in your memory."

"My memory? Mark—he was a great guy."

"Will anyone ever compare?"

"I don't need anyone to compare. I'm not trying to fall in love. I just want someone to do things with every now and then." But oh, she was lying! Right now, right that moment, she could feel herself falling in love with Tyler. Who wouldn't?

He still gazed at her zipper pull. "I've never had a relationship like your marriage. I've never even been close. The women I've gone out with, they've been great—" abruptly he sat back "—but they weren't the type to talk marriage with. So if I don't always look like I understand what you're talking about—when you're remembering everything about marriage—it's because I don't have those experiences."

"But you still want to go out with me? Even though I fired you?"

"I'm glad you fired me. No offense, but I hated being confined to that cubicle."

Remy found herself smiling at that. He really had been a poor fit at Carnegie. However, there were other big differences between them. "I'm forty-two."

"I know. I'm thirty-four."

"That's a pretty big age difference."

"For some people it would be insurmountable. But… not for me." After gazing at her a moment longer, Tyler stood up and walked his glass back to the kitchen.

Remy noticed that it was still half-full. Feeling slightly silly, she stood up and followed him. "Is everything okay?"

"It's perfect." Reaching out, he clasped her hand and pulled. When they were side by side again, he spoke.

"Are you free Monday night? I'd like to take you to dinner."

"I'm free."

"I'm glad. I'll pick you up at seven."

"Do you want to come back and sit down? We could talk some more."

Looking at their linked hands, he shook his head. "To be honest with you, if we go back to that couch, I'm not going to want to talk."

"We could do more than that," she ventured. Yes, she was old. Too old to just sit on the couch and make out. But couldn't they at least neck a little bit?

"Remy, what I want to do needs more than a couch. Let's call it a night." Dropping her hand, he walked to her front door. "I'll see you Monday night at seven."

"I'll be ready."

Very slowly he smiled, flashing his perfect white teeth. "I'll be ready, too."

He turned and left before she could fumble around and say another word. The front door opened and shut. Minutes later she heard his car's powerful engine ignite, then roar away.

Then all that remained was his scent, a half-full glass of wine and the tingling sensation that always pooled in her stomach when she thought of him.

And thought of the way he made her feel.

"SO YOU DIDN'T TAKE HER to bed."

"I'm not going to answer that." Tyler held the fifty-pound bar easily as Keith wiped an already sweaty towel across his brow. Keith had called Sunday morning at seven…supposedly to invite him to work out with him at his fancy gym.

Tyler knew better. He'd called him up on a reconnaissance mission for his wife. Most likely he'd been given strict orders not to come home without plenty of details to share.

But he'd gone ahead with it because he needed to work out. And he wasn't exactly opposed to getting some feedback, either. He was in uncharted waters with this woman. His relationship with Remy was complicated.

So were the feelings she spurred in him.

Keith grinned. "Since you're not going to answer my question...I'm guessing she said no."

"Maybe I didn't ask."

"Why not?"

"She wasn't ready." Eager to hold off another batch of unwanted questions, Tyler pushed the weighty bar toward his brother-in-law. "Do another set of reps or stop," Tyler retorted. "I'm getting tired of holding this damn thing."

Grimly Keith grabbed the bar and slowly brought it to his chest. After exhaling, he pulled it up again. "These never get easier."

"Some things never do."

Such as fending off annoying questions about his personal business. Though, to be fair, Tyler had a feeling any prying he was doing was at the express request of one particularly caring twin sister.

Tyler knew Keith was putty in her hands. At the moment he was searching for information like the most wheedling of girls. It was impressive.

Well, it would have been if it hadn't been so annoying. "So glad Cindy didn't have any problem sharing my personal business with you."

"Did you expect her to?" Keith asked, exhaling as he bench-pressed another three repetitions. "This was a pretty big deal, don't you think? A late-night call soon after firing your butt? She's playing with you, Tyler."

"It wasn't like that. She's not like that."

"Well, she sounds like it. Ramona Greer sounds either desperate or like she's on a power trip."

"She's neither. And don't talk about her like that."

Grabbing the bar, Tyler hung it back on the rack, then led the way to the wall of full-length mirrors, where they each pulled out a set of barbells and began doing biceps curls. A few more men joined their ranks, most lifting the weights with either iPods in their ears or looks of grim determination on their faces.

Keith, however, had no problem chatting away. "What about that girl you sat near at Carnegie? Kaitlyn? Cindy said you've mentioned her a time or two."

"I'm not interested in her."

"You ought to take her out anyway. Take her sailing."

Sailing only made him think about Remy now. "Can't we talk about something else?"

"I can't go home without information, buddy. You know that."

"I hear you," Tyler said as he moved over to a group of mats and sat down. "Okay. Here's the deal. I'm taking Remy out tomorrow night."

"I have a feeling you're making a mistake."

"Then it will be my mistake," he huffed as he began the first of a hundred sit-ups.

"Where are you going to take her?"

"The Polo Grill."

Keith whistled quietly as he joined him on the floor. After doing five stomach crunches, he scowled. "I hate these." After another five, he looked Tyler's way. "The Polo Grill is expensive. Sure you want to go there?"

"Yep."

"How about we join you?"

Tyler paused. So far he'd gotten fifty sit-ups done and every muscle in his belly was starting to burn. "What?"

"You heard me." Keith leaned back against the mirror and watched Tyler continue with his exercise. "How about if we make it a double date? Cindy would love it. And it would neatly stop all the questions."

"I wouldn't enjoy the company. I want to be alone with Remy."

"Come on. It will get us both out of the doghouse."

"I shouldn't even be there. I haven't done anything wrong."

"You moved closer to us. Now everything you do is Cindy's business. I'll make the reservations. Seven?"

"No." Finally finished with his hundred sit-ups, Tyler lay back on the ground and imagined all four of them together. Him trying to hold Remy's hand while his sister and Keith watched them and shot a million questions their way. "I don't want you there."

"How about we'll meet you for drinks first? We'll stay with you one hour, tops. Then you two can go eat your romantic meal and Cindy and I will be on our way."

"I don't know."

"Drinks or dinner…or we're just going to show up."

Unfortunately he could see that happening. "Drinks. But that's it."

"That's enough."

"We'll meet you for cocktails at seven-fifteen at the bar. Then Remy and I will go on our way." Glaring at Keith, he added, "But Lord help you if you say anything to embarrass her. She's a nice woman. And she's a widow."

"I'll be good."

"Tell Cindy, too."

"I will." Keith grinned. "Hallelujah. Now I can go home."

Tyler couldn't help but chuckle. "She wouldn't let you come home without plans, huh? You've got it bad."

"It's called marriage. One day you'll know what I'm talking about."

"I hope so," Tyler murmured before hitting the shower.

Chapter Fourteen

"You didn't have a choice, you know," Shawn said on Monday morning when she met Remy for their weekly meeting.

Completely misreading Remy's agitated state, Shawn started talking about Tyler, obviously trying to make Remy feel better.

Since Remy knew the only thing that would calm her down was seeing Tyler soon, she let Shawn talk. And talk.

"You had to fire Tyler Mann," her assistant continued. "Actually, I'd say he had little to no patience with our customers—I noticed that the first time I listened to one of his calls. It was just a matter of time before he blew a fuse."

"I know." Remy readjusted her reading glasses for about the tenth time that hour. She needed to do anything she could to keep her focus on Tyler at work instead of the Tyler who'd come over and kissed her breathless.

"And he wasn't suited to this job at all." Muffin crumbs littered her blouse as Shawn juggled breakfast and file folders on her lap. "And now that I think about it, Tyler might have been too smart for the job, as well."

Remy pulled off her glasses. "Excuse me?"

"I'm not saying you have to be dumb to work here.

But it's not like we're actively hiring college graduates. The ability to study for exams is not a required skill to answer call-center phones."

Remy took exception to Shawn's explanation. "Over half of our employees have been to college."

"I know. And plenty of the ones who never went are top-notch. Terrific. But that Tyler Mann, he analyzed things. I heard him once questioning a customer's airline schedule and its effect on her business's productivity." She paused, shaking her head at the memory. "Remy, I don't think it's in him to just answer questions without giving his opinion, or trying to make things better. Shoot, a few days ago I heard him speaking with a caller about reevaluating her insurance policies. Remy, he didn't fit in."

"I suppose you're right." Glancing at the clock over her door, Remy slipped on her heels. In a few moments she had another meeting to attend. "Though he did look surprised that I fired him." Of course, he had sure looked pleased about being let go just minutes later....

"I'd be surprised if he hadn't been shocked. I get the feeling that there's very little Tyler Mann hasn't gotten that he's wanted. But look at it this way. If you hadn't let the guy go, people would've questioned you. They would have doubted your leadership abilities. Especially the suits at corporate."

"I know." Taking a deep breath, Remy finally gave up her secret. "I called him on Saturday night."

"To apologize?" Shawn shook her head in wonder. "Remy, you are truly the nicest person I know."

"No...I didn't call him to apologize." Though she was feeling her cheeks heat, Remy continued. She needed some reassurance that she hadn't just turned into a creepy old woman.

She needed to tell someone about how amazing it had been to feel alive again. "Shawn, I called Tyler because I wanted to see him."

"What?"

"I like him." There. She'd said it.

"I had no idea." Shawn shook her head. "Actually, that's not true. I did ask him about sailing, to see if you two went together. But I thought he was pursuing you. Not that it was a mutual thing."

"Oh, it's mutual. I like him, and he likes me, too," Remy added, feeling vaguely like a teenager. "We did have a great time when we went sailing, by the way."

"I see." Shawn popped another chunk of banana muffin into her mouth, obviously still struggling.

As if she was hooked up to a lie detector, Remy added, "That's one of the reasons I hired Tyler, too. I was afraid if I didn't, I'd never see him again."

"That's one way to get acquainted, I guess."

Remy began straightening her desk, readying herself for her next meeting with two employees who had earned bonuses. In marked contrast, Shawn leaned back in her seat and crossed her legs.

Actually, her assistant looked ready to settle in for a long cozy chat in front of a fireplace. "So, what happened when you called?"

"He came over."

With unusual restraint, her assistant kept her voice even and steady. "And...how was that?"

"It was fine. No, better than fine."

"Wow. Things were that good, huh?"

Remy felt her cheeks heat. "I'm not talking about *that*. We didn't...we didn't do much. We ended up talking about my marriage to Mark."

Something new flickered in Shawn's eyes. A new

understanding. Maybe it was a new respect for the very attractive Tyler Mann. "Well, maybe it is time," she said, surprising the heck out of Ramona. "You've done everything you are supposed to do. You married well, you worked hard. You were the best wife you could be to Mark. But now it's time to live a little."

"If things got serious, I don't know what we'd do."

"I do. Y'all would figure things out. Believe me, I wish Eddie and I had talked more and worried a whole lot less about pasts and futures last year. That would have saved us a lot of time and worry…never mind all those lawyer fees."

Ramona started laughing just as a sharp siren rang through the air. "What in the world?"

Shawn scooped up her belongings and hurried to the door. When the siren screamed loudly again, she threw open Remy's door and stepped out into the reception area. A second later she turned to Remy. "It's a fire alarm. Did we have a fire drill scheduled I didn't know about?"

Remy was already on her feet and collecting her purse. "Not at all. Go ahead and get on the loudspeaker and call an evacuation, Shawn. I'll contact Scott—he's the custodian on duty today. I'll dial the fire department, too."

With a quick nod, Shawn scurried to her desk and picked up the phone.

As soon as Remy heard Shawn's voice on the intercom, she dialed the fire department and, after introducing herself, asked, "Any idea what's going on? Could this be a county drill or something?"

"Our indications all say it's a real fire, ma'am," the dispatcher replied, his voice crisp and authoritative.

"Trucks are already on the way. Please direct everyone there to get out."

The next twenty minutes were some of the scariest in her life. Although Carnegie had implemented an evacuation procedure in accordance with federal regulations, and they'd already practiced the procedures twice, nothing prepared Remy for the feelings of loss and panic she was experiencing.

She truly cared about—and felt responsible for—every person in the organization. Like a mother duck, she roamed the area, gently shuffling people up and out of cubicles. With the two-way radio Corporate had given them for emergencies, she was in constant communication with Scott and the rest of the custodial staff, who were evacuating their own personnel, and in charge of checking every bathroom to make sure it was empty.

Scott reported that they'd found the fire—it was in the staff kitchen and break room. It looked large enough that he feared they wouldn't be able to extinguish it without putting workers at risk.

Remy agreed to be cautious, and called the dispatcher back to relay what she'd learned.

The only consolation was that things moved quickly, though it felt like an eternity. People listened and didn't lag. Shawn reported via her own portable radio that everyone who'd exited was standing at the far end of the parking lot as directed.

Finally Remy joined them.

The crowd of people stood in the exact spots they'd been directed to during previous drills—they were on the grassy areas just east of the main parking area. But whereas before, everyone had been chatting and talking, eating snacks and carrying coffee cups, now totes and purses were tightly clasped and an awkward silence filled the air as Remy finally joined the assembled group and watched two fire trucks arrive.

As soon as they pulled to a stop, she rushed forward. Remy hardly did more than introduce herself and give directions to the staff break room before two firefighters in full uniform entered the building.

Her heart felt as if it was lodged in her throat. Oh, she hoped everyone was out and accounted for. It would be devastating if things were worse than they feared and they'd somehow overlooked an employee.

As they waited, a few workers standing nearby asked for information.

"There was a fire in the break room, but I don't know more than that," she admitted. "Let's just hope and pray that it was only in that room and that no one was hurt."

Fifteen minutes later the captain appeared. "Ma'am, you were right. The fire was in the staff kitchen."

"Was anyone there? Do you think everyone's okay?"

"All we found was some building damage, Ms. Greer."

As her heart started beating again, she focused on what they knew. "Any idea what happened?"

"Right now I'd guess the toaster or the oven caused all the damage. Both were pretty charred up. We put it out, and sprayed it good. Currently we're double-checking the walls for sparks and such and making a thorough walk-through to make sure there's not an electrical problem."

"You all arrived so quickly. Thank you."

"No problem. Your security system worked like a charm, by the way. It clicked in and called us. We were on our way when you called it in."

When the captain walked away, Remy forwarded the message to Shawn and Scott, and to the people who'd gathered around.

Twenty minutes later they were given the okay to go back in.

As Scott directed the employees where to go—one of the back hallways was damaged—and Shawn answered questions, Remy met again with the captain. She listened in a daze as he explained a few more things. Now that everyone was safe and the danger had abated, the ramifications began to settle in.

"A toaster did all that damage? That's hard to believe."

The fire captain shrugged. "Stuff happens, you know?"

After placing Shawn in charge of making sure their computer systems were back up and running, Ramona followed the inspector to the break room where, indeed, a real mess awaited her.

The toaster had made enough of a mess that dark sooty stains rose above it and the counter was ruined. She looked at everything in dismay.

Accidents did happen.

After saying goodbye to the men in uniform, Remy allowed herself some time to take a deep breath and refocus. Scott stood by her side, his expression grim. "Ms. Greer, I'm afraid this whole room will have to be gutted and remodeled."

"I think you're right, but that's okay. That's what insurance is for, right?"

"Right."

"What's important is that no one was hurt." Holding out her hands, she reached for Scott's hand. "Thank you so much for your quick thinking and steady, calm demeanor. If people had panicked, we could have been mourning a whole lot more than just a set of kitchen appliances."

"You're welcome. But I have to say we should spread some of the credit around. A bunch of people are talking about Kaitlyn Sinclair. She kept her cool and helped shuffle a whole lot of people out of their cubicles in record time."

"I'm afraid I don't know who Kaitlyn is," Remy admitted. Now that she had Shawn, she focused only on a few employees at a time. If there were no problems with an employee...or if he or she hadn't been marked for a bonus for exceptional performance, she wasn't familiar with them. Especially if they'd been hired over the past year.

"I bet you'll recognize Kaitlyn if you see her." Scanning the people filing back to their cubicles, he pointed her out. "There she is, ma'am. She's the one with all that long blond hair, almost to her waist."

Remy spotted her in an instant. She had noticed her before; she was a beautiful girl. "I see her."

"She's a favorite of mine," Scott said with a smile. "Always has a kind word for everyone. I tried to fix her up with my nephew, but she wasn't having any of it. Said she had her eye on the new guy from Texas."

"Tyler? Tyler Mann?"

"Yeah. He's the guy who just got fired, right?"

"Yes."

"They ate lunch a few times together. I haven't had a chance to ask if they ever went out. I imagine they did, though. I mean, who would turn her down?"

Before she could even attempt to answer that, her

chatty custodian continued. "Hey, maybe now she'll give my nephew another look."

"Maybe so." Swallowing, she tried her best to sound professional. "Thanks, Scott. I'll make sure I speak with Kaitlyn and convey my thanks."

"It's just good no one was hurt." Scott smiled. "And our evacuation procedure worked like a charm!"

"That is something to celebrate," Remy agreed as she wandered back to her office.

She patted shoulders and nodded and smiled at all the employees she passed. No one was answering calls. For once, Remy didn't feel compelled to point out that they had a slew of blinking lights flashing on phones. She knew it was important for everyone to take a deep breath, call their family members and let them know they were okay. Most of the people in the company were professional enough to get back to their jobs after a few moments.

BUT AS SHE WALKED BACK up the stairs to her office, Remy realized that she was thinking about a lot more things than just the company.

Inside, she was reeling from the news about Kaitlyn. Had she and Tyler been dating? Had he been pursuing Remy while spending time with Kaitlyn?

Suddenly she felt old and foolish. Again.

On Saturday night, after Tyler left, she'd spent a good hour on her couch just sitting and daydreaming about him. Planning what she was going to wear for their next date. When she'd finally drifted off to sleep, her mind had focused only on him. How she'd been so lucky to meet someone so special.

She hoped that they both weren't making a big mistake. She sure didn't want to worry that one day he would turn to her and say that he was interested in someone younger.

Because there wouldn't be a single thing she could do about that.

THE REST OF THE DAY passed in a flash. There were forms to fill out, phone calls to return, service orders to take care of. Remy welcomed the chaos and the deluge of business. It all kept her mind off Tyler and away from the crazy mixture of emotions coursing through her. She was embarrassed. Because she'd been falling in love with him.

She should have remembered just how painful love could be. It was time to end things.

She needed to get on the phone right away and break their date.

But simply calling him and breaking things off on the phone didn't sound very brave. She decided to go on this one date, then on the way home tell him that they couldn't see each other anymore. If he asked questions, then she'd answer frankly—tell him how she'd heard someone else had been pursuing him.

She'd explain that while she didn't necessarily have a problem with him dating someone else, she did have a problem with him leading her to believe that he was far more serious than he obviously was.

She would be calm and precise. Unemotional.

Yes, that would be the right way to handle things. It had nothing to do with the fact that a part of her was still looking forward to seeing him. To bask in that smile he sent her direction so well. To pretend, for just a little while, that she was half of a couple.

No longer alone.

Chapter Fifteen

As soon as she got home Remy said goodbye to Carmen, then took a long, hot shower. The pulsating bursts of water eased the knots in her neck and helped her refocus. Next she toweled off and dried and curled her hair. After much deliberation, she decided to pull it back into an uncomplicated ponytail. Someone had once told her she looked younger with it styled simply.

Then, because she wasn't sure where she and Tyler were going, she slipped on black slacks and a loose coral silk top. Gold chandelier earrings and a simple chain completed the outfit.

Well, almost. With a smile, Remy pulled out her impulse purchase from the weekend before. High-heeled black sandals. They were the type of shoes she'd never been able to buy with Mark—she'd never wanted to stand out as taller than him. But with Tyler, the four-inch heels would maybe take her almost to his eye level.

Five minutes after she'd spritzed on perfume, the doorbell rang.

"Am I too early?" Tyler asked the moment she opened the door.

She glanced at her watch. "Not at all. You're right on time. Come in. I've just got to get a purse…." Her voice drifted off as he slid a hand around her waist and brushed his lips against hers. "Oh!"

He obviously enjoyed her bewilderment—his dimple appeared. "Sorry. I couldn't wait. You look beautiful."

"Oh. Well, thank you. You look nice, too." And he did. Wearing a navy blazer over yet another crisp white unbuttoned button-down, he looked as gorgeous as he ever did. Dammit. It was going to be extremely difficult to say goodbye. To have him out of her life.

"So, are you ready?"

For a moment her mind blanked, then she remembered her mission. "I just need to get my purse," she said. "I'll be right back."

"I'll be here," he murmured.

Oh, she hated it when he said things so...so loverlike. When he stared at her as if he didn't want to share her with another person.

When he kissed her as if he couldn't wait to take her to bed. Something visceral happened to her when he did those things. Oh, she was in trouble. They'd been in each other's company only five minutes, but already her knees felt like butter.

He probably made Kaitlyn feel the same way. Remy immediately dismissed that thought, determined to enjoy this last evening with Tyler.

And yet, sitting in his car didn't lessen her tension. Remy was hyper-aware of every move he made. Every mood that flashed across his features.

At the moment he looked pensive.

Worry knotted her stomach as she realized he looked a little tense, too. Maybe he was regretting their date? Maybe he wasn't going to wait until the end to break things off.

Well, better to get things out in the open than keep them secret. "Tyler, is everything okay?"

"Maybe." His lips pursed as he gripped the steering wheel. "I've got something to tell you, but I don't know how you're going to take it."

"Oh?" Her stomach sank.

He grimaced. "I almost called you earlier. But I didn't want to take a chance that you'd cancel. But I think I should have called. It would have been better."

Well, there it was. He was definitely going to end things. She was too old. He'd found someone else. This was some kind of awkward last date. "Maybe you should just tell me what you need to tell me," she said tightly. "Then we'll both stop worrying."

"Okay. But promise you'll hear me out before getting mad."

The waiting was fraying her nerves. "Tyler, what is it?"

Instead of answering, he darted a look her way again. "Remy, do you promise to hear me out?"

"Yes! I promise. What?"

"We don't have reservations right at seven-fifteen. They're at eight."

Remy swallowed hard. Huh?

Tyler continued. "Actually, the reason I changed our reservation is because…I promised my brother-in-law that he and Cindy could meet us for drinks before dinner."

She still was having trouble getting her mind around his words. This was his big announcement? Not that he was about to break up with her? "What?"

"My sister and brother-in-law want to meet you and they wouldn't take no for an answer. I'm really sorry."

"Oh."

"Oh? You aren't mad?"

She felt like laughing. "No. I thought you were going to say you didn't want to see me anymore."

He looked stunned. "Why would you think that? I've been following you around like a puppy since we first met, begging you to give me a chance."

Feeling somewhat embarrassed, she decided to get everything out in the open. "Tyler, see, I thought you were going to tell me that you were dating Kaitlyn."

"Kaitlyn?" After a moment he looked her way again, shock transforming his features. "The girl at work? Why?"

She lifted a hand to her brow, brushing a stray curl that had escaped her ponytail, then said, "Someone at work told me y'all were close...."

"We sat close to each other."

Seeking to sound way more calm and collected than she felt, she said, "It's okay if you two got close. I mean, we never made any commitments...."

Tyler was so stunned, he was thankful they were at a stoplight. He needed a moment to gather his thoughts and formulate a response. "Kaitlyn's nice. I'm sure she'll make someone a great girlfriend. But no, we're not dating."

Slowly she said, "You're telling me the truth, aren't you? You're not dating her."

"Remy, I'm sorry, but I'm amazed that you'd think that. And I'm more than a bit surprised that you listened to office gossip."

She bit her lip and a tiny guilty look sprouted between her brows. "I wouldn't put it that way."

He chuckled. "I would. Haven't you read the handbook lately, Ms. Greer? Page seventy-two talks all about how gossip can be detrimental to a positive work environment."

The light turned and he was forced to focus on the road. But the traffic wasn't enough to sidetrack his mind.

"I'm sorry I even brought it up. It's a girl thing, I guess. Kaitlyn is pretty."

"She is pretty. But she's not you." He almost told her why he'd come to Carnegie. Almost told her that he dreamed about her the way thirteen-year-olds dreamed of being the star pitcher, or the lead singer in a band. But that would really send her running. "So you're not mad about drinks with my sister?"

"No. I think it's kind of cute. I just hope they'll approve."

"They will." But he couldn't care less if they did or not. He'd never been the type to rely on other people for approval—not even his sister. "It's just an hour, then we'll have our date," he said as he pulled into the Polo Grill's parking lot.

The restaurant had valet parking, but he ignored it, uneager to share Remy's presence with anyone else. After he turned off the ignition, he leaned over and kissed her. Lightly.

And then it began again. One kiss became another. That one became incredible. So deep. So hot.

Lifting his head, he smiled as Remy pressed her fingers to her mouth. "Oh, my lipstick. Shoot. They'll know what we've been doing. Can you wait a sec while I fix myself up?"

"I can wait all day."

Tyler felt almost smug as he exited, then walked around the car to her side. When he opened her door she was ready, and looked at him with a smile. "So, do we need a sign?" she said as she very femininely held out a hand for him to assist her.

He kept hold of her hand as they walked the short distance to the restaurant's entrance. "What do you mean?"

"Mark and I used to have a sign, a call sign or signal to use in situations like this. If things got too uncomfortable or awkward, one of us would say the word and the other used to come to the rescue."

"I like that idea." He also liked that she was bringing up her ex-husband without the usual pain in her voice. Trying to think of something unusual, he recalled a pair of men playing a game on the boardwalk the other day. "How about Parcheesi?"

"Parcheesi?" Scorn filled her tone. "You're obviously new at this. Parcheesi will not do. Tyler, it has to be something that would come up in normal conversation… like *coffee* or *sunset.*"

Enjoying the idea of the two of them having a little private signal, he thought again. "I know—the word is *sailing,*" he murmured, liking that word a whole lot more than he ever used to. Sailing now reminded him of their first date, of kissing her for the first time. "If things get bad, say something about sailing and I'll rescue you."

Her lips curved. "Promise?"

"Definitely," he said as he opened the door and let the hostess lead them to the bar.

Where Cindy and Keith were already waiting.

Feeling vaguely as if they were going into battle, Tyler said, "That's them over there. I promise, this will be fine. They're nice."

He sure hoped it was true.

CINDY LOOKED A LOT LIKE Tyler, Remy reflected as they approached the couple, who were now standing. Same black hair. Same dark eyes. Tall. Keith was a study in contrast—blond hair, blue eyes. He looked a little like Barbie's Ken, though less perfect and more cuddly.

"Hi. Ramona Greer."

"Cindy Westbridge. This is my husband, Keith."

After they got settled and the cocktail waitress came by, Remy had the unmistakable impression she was being examined. Next to her, Tyler seemed a little tense.

Remy instinctively knew it was because he felt protective about her, not that he was afraid she'd do something wrong. And because she now felt a little more sure of her relationship with him—at least she knew he wasn't dating Kaitlyn—she attempted to put him at ease. "You know, in all the years that I've lived here, I've never been to this restaurant. Do you two come here a lot?"

"Pretty much never," Cindy replied. "We have two kids, you know."

"I've met April. Tyler and I ran into each other at Movies and More. She is so cute."

Cindy raised an eyebrow. "I didn't hear about that."

"It was when I had April overnight," he explained.

"Tyler was stocking up on Baby Einstein."

"Oh, yes, now I remember. Oh, boy, that was a weekend and a half. Megan was sick. I think it took me a whole week to recover!" Looking her over, Cindy smiled. "Of course, I wouldn't trade one moment of motherhood for anything. Have, uh, you ever thought about having kids one day?"

Well, the interrogation had begun in record time. The question was a painful one, but Cindy couldn't know that. Doing her best to keep her composure, Remy said, "I have."

"In your former marriage—"

"Cindy…" Tyler's voice held an unmistakable warning.

"It's okay," Remy murmured. "My former marriage was cut short because my husband had lung cancer. We didn't think the timing was right for children." Though that wasn't why they'd never had children. She had been the one with the problem in that department—to her shame.

But it wasn't anyone's business.

Cindy closed her eyes for a moment. When she opened them, pure repentance was in her gaze. "I'm sorry. I never should have asked such a thing. I promise, I'm not usually so rude."

Tyler reached for Remy's hand and gave it a gentle, reassuring squeeze. "Maybe we should talk about something else. Like sailing, Remy?"

She almost smiled. "Not yet."

This time it was Keith who looked confused. "You only talk about sailing at certain times?"

Sipping her wine, Remy shook her head. "No, only when I'm feeling uncomfortable. But I'm okay." She stopped herself from saying anything else. She couldn't help her age or her childless state. She couldn't help that Tyler liked her. She'd come too far to risk falling apart over things she couldn't help.

A new appreciation filled Keith's tone when he spoke again. "Has Tyler ever told you a twin story?"

"No. I didn't know there was such a thing."

Cindy laughed. "Back when we were small, we got into a lot of trouble together."

"Especially at school," Tyler said.

"How? The only twin stories I've heard were like *The Parent Trap,* where twins traded places."

Looking fondly at her brother, Cindy said, "We'd

gang up on people. Teachers. Mom and Dad. You name it."

"We were a united force. And when we both wanted something, it was a pretty tough opposition."

Remy was charmed. "Were y'all ever in the same class?"

"Once." Eyes full of mischief over her pink cosmopolitan, Cindy looked at her brother. "Remember poor Mrs. Walker?"

"I could never forget. We were so mean to her." Explaining, Tyler added, "One day we told the biggest fib to our teacher. Saying that we were home alone and our parents were in Paris."

"Never realizing that maybe it would be illegal for parents to leave two seven-year-olds alone."

"We really had her going, talking about our food supply and our to-do list."

"The principal, too."

Remy leaned forward. "What happened?"

"Unbeknownst to us, the principal called all the people on our emergency forms and asked them to come for a meeting."

"Then all hell broke loose," Tyler said with a grimace. "Our neighbor called Mom, wanting to know why the big important meeting was scheduled. Mom called Dad...."

"And at two o'clock, everyone arrived," Cindy said with a shudder.

"I can't believe I've never heard this story," Keith interjected.

"I can," Cindy quipped. "I've never been in a hurry to share it, honey. It wasn't our finest hour."

Tyler chuckled. "So Cindy and I tromp into the principal's office, sure the administrator felt so sorry for us that we might get an extra ice cream from the cafeteria."

"But that didn't happen?"

"Oh, no. Everyone was there, half arguing, half complaining. And then they all glared at us."

"It was horrible," Cindy confirmed. "We got yelled at by so many people, they were practically waiting in line for their turn."

"The ride home was even worse. Dad kept talking about respect and honesty." Looking at his sister, Tyler smiled. "He pretty much said we were sadly lacking in both qualities."

"Mom kept nodding and repeating everything Dad said. When all was said and done, we got no ice cream for two weeks."

Remy shared an amused smile with Keith. "Oh. My. That was harsh punishment indeed."

"It felt like it," Tyler said as he squeezed her hand again.

"That wasn't the worst part," Cindy said. "The worst was we were separated for a whole week. We couldn't sit together to study or to watch cartoons."

"And we had to write apology notes to everyone." With a grimace, Tyler shook his right hand. "I can still feel the cramp in my hand from writing those."

"Each one had to have five lines and be in cursive," Cindy explained.

Remy thought it really was amazing how they seemed to read each other's minds and could finish each other's sentences without missing a beat.

Remy laughed. "Your poor parents."

"We drove them crazy, I'm sure." Sobering, Cindy looked at Tyler. "But then one day they were gone."

Keith rubbed his wife's shoulder. "So...can't we talk sailing yet?"

"What do you think, Remy?" Tyler murmured as he slowly rubbed a thumb over her knuckles. "Ready to talk sailing now?"

"Not at all. I haven't enjoyed a story so much in months. I think I'd be a fool to pass up hearing another one."

"Maybe another time." As Tyler glanced at his watch, Remy noticed he looked almost sad. "But gosh, it's eight o'clock. We better go claim our table."

"But wait a minute." Cindy grabbed her purse and looked ready to stand up. "We have a babysitter for another three hours. Keith and I could join you now."

Tyler didn't even try to look as if he was interested in that idea. "I don't think so."

Keith chuckled. "I had a feeling you'd say that."

"Well, I sure didn't." Cindy frowned.

Before Remy could think of something to say to settle the light argument, Tyler spoke again. "This has been fun, but I asked Remy out for dinner. With just me. I'm sure you understand."

Once again, her insides turned to jelly. She knew the right thing to do would be to invite Keith and Cindy to join them.

But...she didn't want to. The tension and attraction and mixed-up, crazy nerves that had been festering between them for so long were rolling to a boil, and frankly, she had no desire to have anyone witness it.

Cindy wasn't happy. "Honestly, Ty—"

Keith took one look at the two of them and obviously saw something his wife overlooked. "We've got other plans, anyway."

"We do? What?"

"It's a surprise." Cupping Cindy's elbow, Keith smiled at Remy. "It was nice to meet you."

"It was nice to meet you both," Remy replied.

Tyler waggled three fingers. "Bye, now."

Cindy's farewell was barely heard as Keith shuffled her out of the bar.

Chuckling, Remy turned to Tyler. "Do you think they really did have somewhere else to go?"

"Nope." He leaned closer. Reached out and gently hooked a stray strand of hair behind an ear. "But I hope for Keith's sake they find something open soon. My sister did not look happy."

"I think that had more to do with you."

"I know it did." Looking boyishly pleased, Tyler said, "But I'm not sorry. You look beautiful. I don't want to look at anyone else."

Oh, what a line. It should have sounded cheesy. Trite. Ridiculous. So why was she so pleased to hear it?

Why were her insides turning to mush?

Again?

Chapter Sixteen

They'd had lobster. Oysters. Macadamia coconut ice cream. A crisp pinot grigio. Every course had been excellent, and the servers had been great—somehow knowing when to approach them and when to give them privacy.

The ambience in the restaurant had been warm and romantic. The candles on the tables had flickered against the fine linen tablecloths, and the view from each window had been spectacular.

Together they'd watched the sun fade into the Gulf, bleeding into the water. For an instant the difference between sky and sea had been blurred. Remy had held Tyler's hand and sighed, as if it was the most magical thing she'd ever seen.

For a moment Tyler had been ready to take all the credit for the service, the food, the sunset—anything to impress Remy. Anything to keep that shining look of promise in her eyes.

Two hours later, when they returned to his Corvette, she smiled. "Thank you for dinner."

"It was my pleasure." He paused at the street, unsure where they were going. Somehow none of their conversation had centered around the rest of the night. "Where to? There's a bar on the pier that's kind of fun." He couldn't really care less about it, but he sure wasn't ready to say good-night.

"I'm not really up for another bar."

"Oh." He thought quickly. "The beach? We could go for a walk."

"Not in these shoes. Maybe you could just take me home?"

"Sure." Disappointment coursed through him, though he fought it back. There was no need to rush things. She'd been a good sport about Cindy and Keith. And their meal had been excellent. She'd looked relaxed and amused. As if she could be in his company for hours. He'd loved that.

In addition, it was very likely they'd be going out again, soon. So taking her home was no problem. He'd kiss her good-night and call her in the morning. That was enough.

But then he looked at her.

Promise shone in her eyes. His pulse beat a little faster. It was no trouble at all to push on the accelerator.

When they entered her home, he pulled her into his arms and touched his lips to hers. When she pressed closer, he slid his hands from her waist to her hips. She felt just how he'd imagined. Feminine. Soft.

Carefully he tilted his head, nibbled her bottom lip, then, as she pressed closer, Tyler finally opened his lips and tasted her. Then did it again. Remy moaned and responded in kind. She pressed one hand against his back, and with the other combed fingers through the hair on the nape of his neck.

It was only natural to cup a breast then. He pressed his lips to her cheek, her jaw. She twisted to let him have greater access. Never one to pass up a good opportunity, he complied, feeling her curves, enjoying how easily she responded to his touch.

There was no artifice in her responses, no hesitancy in her touch. It was so sweet.

Eager for more, he pulled her blouse away from the waistband of her pants. Enjoyed how soft and smooth her midriff was. She moved closer, teetered on her heels, then gasped.

Their connection ended. With another gasp, she pulled away. "Wow."

"Yeah." He was breathing deeply. If he'd been home, if he'd been with someone else, he'd have begun the long walk to his bed. But she was special.

And she was a widow and had been with no one since her husband. So he waited. *Come on, Remy,* he silently urged. *Tell me what you want.*

Stepping closer, she looked about to speak, but then her ankle wobbled. To steady herself, she placed a hand on his shoulder. "You okay?" he asked.

"Yes, but I almost sprained my ankle." Lifting one foot out in front of her, she grimaced. "I knew I shouldn't have worn these shoes. They're new and they're nothing but trouble. I think they've already given me two blisters." As she pointed her toe experimentally, her lips curved. "I just couldn't help myself, though. They're so pretty."

In truth, he hadn't noticed them much, only how her legs had looked in the higher heel. "Why don't you take them off?"

A moment passed. Looking vulnerable, she met his gaze again. "They've got straps. I need to sit down to remove them. Do you want to come to the living room?"

"Sure." There it was. He fought back a wave of

disappointment. She was definitely not inviting him to her bed. Not tonight.

But she wasn't kicking him out just yet, either.

Recalling how many hours he'd sat in his cubicle his first day of work, wondering how he was going to even manage another five-minute conversation with her, he figured things weren't bad after all.

To celebrate the feeling, he scooped her up in his arms, feeling only mildly silly. "Tyler, what are you doing?"

"Carrying you."

"You don't need to. My ankle's fine!"

"Maybe I like feeling you in my arms."

Her cheeks stained red. "I don't believe you—"

"Believe it. I promise, it gets better." Just to hear her laugh, he twirled her around once, then unceremoniously plopped her down on the couch. "Here you go."

She laughed as she landed with a thud. "Remind me never to let you carry me again. Your landings need some improvement."

"I'll work on them if you let me pick you up again."

A spark of promise, of awareness, lit her eyes. "So, want to sit down?" Remy patted the cushion next to her.

He sat. When she bent to unbuckle the thin leather strap of her shoe, he waved her hands away. "Let me help you." To his delight, she didn't hesitate. Slowly she placed her foot on his thigh.

The leather was supple and unbuckled easily. After he tossed down the shoe, he did the same with the other one. When she tried to remove her feet from his lap, he held firm. "No way. I'm keeping you here for a moment." Expertly he rubbed the arches of her feet, calming the bunched muscles.

When she relaxed, he laid them on the couch and then slid on top of her.

Remy's hands curved around his shoulders. "What are you doing?"

"I'm going to kiss you for a little bit. Do you have a problem with that?"

"No. I mean…do you mind if we don't go to bed? Tonight?"

"Tonight" meant she wanted to in the future. And any future with her was worth waiting for. "I don't mind at all. As long as you stop talking. Just let me kiss you. Just let me kiss you the way I've been dying to."

She answered by arching her back and meeting his mouth. Tenderly stroking his lips with her tongue, she nibbled a bit, then darted her tongue inside. With a groan, he let her set the pace, letting her deepen their kisses, pausing for a breath, smiling when she tilted her head so he could trace her jaw with his tongue.

Then it was only natural to push down the spaghetti straps of her coral blouse and help her unfasten the row of tiny buttons.

Just underneath was a matching coral bra. He'd just shifted a bit so he could admire the play of coral against her skin, enjoying the faint outline of her nipples underneath the almost sheer fabric, when she surprised him and unhooked the front clasp.

She smiled when he looked at her in surprise. "I may want to take things a little slow, Tyler, but I still want you."

"You take off as much as you want, as slowly as you want," he murmured as he got to know her breasts. "Believe me, I like our pace just fine."

As he tenderly licked at a nipple, she moaned a bit

and pulled his head closer, inviting him to do all kinds of good things.

Luckily, no further discussion was necessary.

Chapter Seventeen

"We like her," Cindy proclaimed when Tyler came over for dinner on Tuesday night. "Just wanted you to know."

Tyler pressed a kiss to his twin's forehead on the way to their spare refrigerator in the garage. After pulling out a pair of sodas, he handed one to his sister before sitting in front of April's high chair.

His tiny niece kicked her heels in greeting, her pudgy hands occupied with a graham cracker mess in her hands.

"I think your mommy sounds surprised, Miss April," Tyler cooed. "I think she thought I was dating some dirty old woman."

April squealed and thrust a corner of the mushy graham back into her mouth.

After checking on the French fries baking in the oven, Cindy joined them. "I didn't think that."

"But you almost did."

"Okay. I'll admit I was a little skeptical."

"A little? Cindy, don't you remember your 'young love' lecture? You were a *lot* skeptical."

"That's because on paper she seemed all wrong for you."

Since he'd first become intrigued with Remy because

of an article written on paper, he felt differently. However, he wanted—and needed—Cindy's good wishes for his new relationship. He moved to Destin to become closer with his sister. He sure didn't want Remy to pull them apart. "But what about in person? How did you feel about Remy then?"

"In person…she was great. And, darn it, she's beautiful, too. I hope I look that good at forty-two."

Tyler couldn't help but smile at his sister's comment. The way she was talking, someone would think that Remy was on social security. "Since you're only eight years younger, I'm going to predict that you'll be beautiful, too."

Cindy rolled her eyes as she sipped from her orange soda. "Remy's got an amazing figure, too." Looking at her stomach, she frowned. "Of course, I think things are easier to keep in place if you've never had children."

Tyler wasn't going to touch that one. "I'll take your word for it."

"But…do you think Remy wants kids?"

"I'm sure she does. You should have seen her with April at Movies and More. She could hardly stop looking at her."

April kicked her feet and spat out a chunk of graham for emphasis. Cindy laughed as she strode to the kitchen and grabbed a paper towel, dampening it quickly before wiping down her daughter. "What a mess this little stinker is. Remy might think differently about having a houseful of babies if she saw what they were like, all covered in goo."

"I doubt soggy grahams would faze her in the slightest. I think she'll be a great mom." He held out his hands as Cindy pulled a wiped-down April out of the high chair, unfastened her bib and handed her to him.

Right away April smiled and started playing with the buttons on his shirt. "Cin, did you notice how much April likes me now? I think we bonded when she spent the night with me."

"I bet she did. I still can't believe you volunteered to watch her. Oh, Ty, I would've been a nutcase if you hadn't been here. I sure hope you won't have to move to find another job."

"That's nothing you need to worry about. I've got plenty of money in the bank. Plenty of time to look for something new."

"Something better than Carnegie."

"Something a lot better." As he cuddled April, enjoying the feel of the contented baby in his arms, he said, "Things are working out, don't you think? I'm dating a gal who's wonderful, and she's never going to leave here." Already he could imagine one day in the future, with Remy heavy with child, and all of them gathering for a barbecue or a holiday.

His life was going to be everything he'd imagined when he'd decided to move away from Houston. Everything he wanted—family, babies, a future—was worth any sacrifice.

He couldn't wait until he was sure Remy was ready, too.

BLAMING A HEADACHE, Remy left Carnegie early on Tuesday, something she usually never did. But, things were out of sorts at the call center. Fire inspectors and insurance agents had visited twice since the fire. Now work crews were busy in the kitchen, pulling down old cabinets and laminate and bringing in new materials. The noise echoed through the building.

But work wasn't all that occupied her thoughts. Far

more on her mind were the latest developments with Tyler. So much had happened between them over the past few days, she knew she was going to explode if she didn't take some time for herself to recap and regroup.

She decided to go home and enjoy the day. Outside, the air was a balmy eighty-five. Perfect for a swim and then a little lying about. She always enjoyed taking some time to stretch muscles and just enjoy the day.

As soon as she got home she said hello to Carmen, pulled on her favorite black one-piece, grabbed sunscreen and a pair of white fluffy towels, then strode out to the pool.

Moments later all the past week's tension seemed to evaporate as she did a shallow dive into the end of the pool, surfaced a few yards beyond, then began a slow, methodical freestyle. Over the next three or four laps she'd increase the speed, but for now, she wearily allowed her mind to quiet as she merely concentrated on putting one arm over the other.

Thirty-five minutes later, her body relaxed and her mind less confused, she lay down on one of the deck chairs and finally allowed her mind to drift to Tyler. Again.

And last night.

No, they hadn't quite made love. But things had gotten heated. No, she hadn't proclaimed her everlasting love to him, or even talked about a future, but their relationship had definitely taken a big step forward.

The truth was evident. She liked him. She liked him a lot, enough to stop worrying so much about what others would think, or what people at work would think.

Or what Mark would think…though she already had a good idea what he would say. No doubt about it, he'd smile and say something like *Good for you. It's about time.*

And he would be right.

Mark had always been about living for now, and for taking chances. He'd been so glad he'd built their extravagant house. That they'd gone to St. Thomas for their honeymoon. That he'd played golf as much as he did, and that he'd played at the exclusive country club nearby.

He'd loved learning to scuba dive, and he'd never regretted having dinner with his parents every Wednesday night. "I don't have regrets," he'd told her the day they'd moved him back home from the hospital. The day everyone involved had finally come to terms with the fact that he was never going to get better. The day she'd let him come home to die. "I wouldn't be able to find peace if I did."

She'd held on to those words for weeks after his death. Now they echoed in her heart, reverberated again and again, reminding her how life was fragile and shouldn't be taken for granted.

Funny how she'd forgotten all that. Until Tyler had appeared in her life, she had been doing the very thing she'd vowed not to do. She'd been on autopilot. Forgetting how to live.

Forty-five minutes later Carmen appeared, a glass of iced tea in her hand. "I thought you might like something cold to drink," she said, walking along the pool deck in her white tennis shoes.

"Thanks. It's warmer out here than it looks."

"Especially in that black bathing suit." Looking her over, Carmen frowned. "Señora Greer, I thought you were going to buy something sexy."

"I did. But a bikini is not the thing to wear when swimming laps."

Still looking at her suit as if it covered Remy from neck to ankle, Carmen clucked. "I suppose not."

Sitting up a bit, Remy looked over at her friend. There was something new in Carmen's voice. Something that sounded a little defeated. "Hey, are you okay? You sound a little blue."

Carmen shrugged as she sat in the chair next to Remy's, the one that was thankfully under the shade of a lapis blue umbrella. "I am a bit blue, I admit. Marisol is unhappy with her accounting job."

"When did she tell you that?" This was a big deal, Remy knew. It was a point of pride that Carmen had worked fifty and sixty hours a week while her daughter Marisol got her accounting degree from the nearby community college.

Carmen had thrown a huge party when Marisol graduated. Though it hadn't been too long after Mark had passed on, Remy had made sure she'd attended. The college degree was the first in Carmen's family, and the whole family had beamed with pride when showing off the graduation program, the diploma and the best news of all—the fact that Marisol had landed a job at Meriwether and Fink, one of the biggest accounting firms in the area.

"She sat Miguel and me down last night and told us that she was unhappy. That she was thinking about quitting."

"Oh, my."

"*Sí.*" She nodded. "For a moment I thought Miguel was going to stand up and start screaming at our sweet daughter."

That was a shock. Carmen's husband, Miguel, was as mild mannered as they came. "But he didn't?"

"No. But I did." Covering her eyes, Carmen shook her head in dismay. "I couldn't help myself, you know? I told her I didn't understand her thinking. That she sounded spoiled."

"Uh-oh."

"You're right. It didn't go over too well. But Señora Greer, I know I'm right. I mean, why does she need to be happy at work? She has a good job."

Remy tried to tread carefully. In her world, she knew of many people who changed occupations every few years, who went back to school in their forties. Who needed to be happy and fulfilled in whatever job they held. However, she knew Carmen didn't necessarily understand such a way of thinking. She and Miguel had had plenty of jobs they didn't enjoy to provide for their children—to give them a better life.

"How did things end?"

"I told her I would think about what she told us." Wringing her hands, Carmen added, "I think there's more to this. I think she's dating a boy who's not Catholic. Who might not even be Latino."

"Have you met him?"

"I have not." Despair filled her voice.

"Maybe you should? I don't have kids, but I remember thinking my parents never understood where I was coming from. But when they tried to understand, I tried to listen to them, too."

"I want her dating someone from *our* community. From *our* church. There's plenty of nice men for her to pick from. She's just being stubborn."

Remy sipped her tea. Carmen had been a wonderful friend to her for years. She'd listened to Remy cry and worry like no one else. So she'd sit with her friend for as long as she wanted and listen. And she'd try her best to understand Carmen's point of view.

But she didn't know how she could help.

"Señora Greer, I was thinking maybe you could talk to her," Carmen blurted.

Caught off guard, Remy hastily put her iced tea back on the side table. "Me? I don't know what I'd tell her."

"I do. You could tell her how nice it is to be in a good job. How nice it is to have people working for you. That she needs to stay where she is. She'll listen to you. She respects you, Señora Greer."

"Carmen, I'd do anything for you, but I don't know if Marisol would care about what I'd have to say."

"She would. She admires you. You're a business-woman."

"I bet she admires you even more, Carmen," Remy said slowly. "Just like I admire you. You're a wonderful mother. You've done so much for her."

Carmen waved off her words with a hand. "My advice isn't what she needs. Please, would you talk to her?"

"Well, of course I will. If that's what you want."

Pure relief shone in her eyes. "*Gracias*. I'll tell her to stop by sometime this week after work. Then you could talk about the business world."

Carmen's words triggered an idea. "What would you think if I asked Tyler to speak with her? He's switched jobs, and knows a lot more than I do about making career changes. All I've done is go up the ladder at Carnegie."

For a moment her housekeeper beamed. "Ah, your Tyler is back?"

"Actually…yes."

"Having him speak to Marisol would be fine with me.

Anything to get my daughter back on track." Carmen stood up. "*Bien*. I'll go call her and tell her to stop by."

"I can't wait," Remy replied, though she doubted Carmen heard her. The other lady was already making her way back to the house.

As she lay back down and closed her eyes, Remy fought a smile. Well, that's what happened when you didn't want to think about something—a whole batch of new problems appeared.

She just hoped Tyler wouldn't balk at offering career advice to a twenty-four-year-old.

Chapter Eighteen

"So you wouldn't mind speaking to Carmen's daughter?" Remy asked as soon as Tyler walked in her front door. "I know it's not really your thing, but maybe you could help."

"I don't know much about employment advice, but I'm happy to help," he said as he leaned close and kissed her hello. "I told you I would, remember?"

"I remember." Smiling up at him, Remy couldn't believe how content she felt. How happy and right. She was so glad they'd gotten over their problems and could now just enjoy each other's company.

After some thought, Remy had decided that their meeting with Marisol should take place on their back patio. It was shady and cool, and not too formal. More than anything, she wanted Carmen's daughter to feel at ease. While leading Tyler to the patio, she said, "Actually, Tyler, I think you know more than you might realize. And you've got a good idea about the whole business community. I just worked my way up through the ranks of Carnegie."

"And what does she want?"

"I'm not sure, but I think she's wondering what else she can do with her accounting degree. Carmen said she's taken a job at a big firm and she's not happy."

"Those big firms can be tough. There's a lot of office politics involved that a young lady might not be too comfortable with. I happen to know quite a few business owners out here from my previous life in sales. I'd be happy to visit with her, and if I think she might be a good match, I'll try to help her get some interviews."

Remy was impressed with how much thought he was putting into the upcoming conversation, as well as his true willingness to help a total stranger. Tyler really was a great guy. "This is working out far better than I'd even imagined," she said happily.

Smiling at her enthusiasm, Tyler said, "To be honest with you, I'm kind of looking forward to the opportunity. I'm not used to only sitting around and working on my tan."

This was why she liked him so much. Tyler was so unassuming. Modest. And helpful. Pressing a kiss to his cheek, she said, "Thank you again."

"Oh, no. If you're going to thank me, you need to do it properly." And with that, Tyler pulled her into his arms and kissed her as if there was nothing else in the world at all.

Which, at the moment, Remy was pretty sure was a fact. All too soon the front doorbell rang and she scurried to answer it—sincerely hoping she didn't look as flushed and flustered as she felt.

TYLER LIKED Marisol Rodriguez the instant they met. He liked her curly black hair and ready smile. He thought her slender build looked elegant and classy in her casual shirtwaist dress and sandals. But what really impressed him was the determination he saw in her eyes. This was a woman who knew what she wanted…and was willing to make sacrifices in order to achieve those goals.

After Remy served them both iced tea, cheese and crackers, she left them, frankly telling Marisol that she thought Tyler would be a better person to offer advice than she was.

When they were alone, Tyler decided to be direct, too. "First, I want you to know I'm only speaking to you because your mother asked me to. I would ordinarily never dare to get into your business."

"I understand," the girl replied, but everything in her body language told Tyler a different story. She had stopped by because she was a good daughter, but she didn't appreciate her mother's heavy-handed interference—or anyone else's. "However, I should let you know that my mind is made up. No matter what you say about it, I'm still going to quit soon."

"I figured that."

"Really?"

"Really. You're exactly right—it's none of my business whether you work for an accounting firm or not. But since I used to sell software to a large number of businesses in the area, I thought I might be able to help you decide where you want to apply. Now, what, exactly, do you want to do instead of accounting?"

Marisol shrugged. "Something to do with people. You can't imagine how boring it is to deal with numbers all day. I want to talk to customers, deal with their problems. Make a difference."

Tyler didn't even attempt to hide his smile.

Marisol glared at his grin. "It's not funny."

"I know it's not. It's just that I can completely sympathize with your feelings. Dealing with customers is not as easy as one might think, though."

"But still." She shrugged. "My *madre* doesn't understand. She thinks I should only work at one place until I retire."

"Are you sure that's all she wants from you?"

She had the grace to look embarrassed. "No."

"But…"

Marisol rolled her eyes. "But she's driving me crazy. My mother is beside herself with worry about my future."

"Why don't you tell me about what you studied in college, and what kind of job you hope to have."

The pretty brunette didn't need any further coaching. In no time, Marisol launched into a brief history of her efforts in college, the various internships she'd completed and her grade point average. "It's not that I'm not happy to have a good job," Marisol added. "It's just that I'm not happy there."

"Ah."

That one word led Marisol to start speaking again. In no time, Tyler heard about her drive to please her father and her dissatisfaction at work. Through it all, Marisol described how disappointed she was with being so professionally unfulfilled.

Her words sparked some ideas. Pulling over the little pad of paper she had out, Tyler helped himself to her pencil and started jotting down notes. "Let's broaden your focus," he said. "What do you see yourself doing in five years?"

From the kitchen, Remy listened attentively. She was so glad she'd asked Tyler to speak with Marisol, and was really impressed with the way he conducted their conversation. He asked pointed questions, provided positive feedback and encouraged Marisol to expand on her ideas.

He was a pro at career management.

She'd seen his résumé. She'd called his references, and understood that he'd been extremely successful in the software industry. But now she realized that he had potential to inspire that productivity in other people, as well.

It made her feel even prouder and more special to be his girlfriend.

His girlfriend. She shook her head at the label. It worked. Who would have thought?

After a few more minutes, when it sounded as if they were simply chatting, Remy joined them again.

"So, have you two come up with any ideas?"

Already Marisol looked more relaxed. "I didn't realize it, but there are other ways I can use my degree than just by working in an accounting firm. I could work for the city, or with a small business just starting out."

Tyler nodded. "Marisol seems to have a good head on her shoulders. Marisol, if you'd like, I could look around a bit and help you apply to some places. We'll work on your résumé, too."

"But what about my job now?"

"You keep it. Anyone who's been around the block will tell you that even a bad job is worse than no job. And you don't have a bad one."

"It's just boring."

"I bet the paycheck isn't. I have to agree with your mom and dad on this one. Don't overlook the benefits of being able to afford your lifestyle. In this day and age, too many people would love to have your problems."

"All right," Marisol said meekly.

"Here's my card. That's my cell phone. Call me when you're ready to work on that résumé."

"I can't thank you enough. I think my parents will listen and approve of this plan."

"And you do, too?" Remy asked. She sure didn't want them talking Marisol into anything she didn't want to do.

"Definitely. We were about to have world war three at my house."

Remy stood up. "Now, your mom wanted me to mention this boy you're dating...."

Instantly Marisol's guard went up. "Yes?"

Remy winked. "I've done that, right? I've mentioned him?"

Pure relief filled the young woman's features as she realized Remy wasn't even going to attempt to pry into her love life. "Oh, yes, Ms. Greer. You've mentioned him, and that's enough for me."

"For me, too," Remy said as she ushered Marisol out. "I'm glad you stopped by."

Whispering close, Marisol said, "Ms. Greer, is Tyler really your boyfriend?"

It was time to come out of the closet. "Yes." She held her breath as Marisol glanced at him again. Told herself that it didn't matter what the twenty-four-year-old thought.

"He's great," Marisol said finally. "You two look great together, too."

"Thanks."

When she came back in, Tyler wasn't waiting for her in the living room. She spied him just beyond, outside on the porch in back of the kitchen.

"Do you ever use your pool?" he asked as she joined him.

"I do. I swim laps a few times a week."

"I didn't know that. I wonder why I didn't?" he mused.

Resting her arms on the iron bar of the balcony, she said, "Probably the same reason I didn't know you were so savvy about employment advice."

Delight lit his eyes. "Marisol liked what I said?"

"She did. I did, too." She paused. "I'm so glad you stopped by. Carmen asked me to talk to her, but all I could think of was to tell her to keep her job."

"Glad I could help."

"You ought to do something with that skill."

"What skill?"

"Career planning."

"Remy, are we going to talk about work right now? Because I sure don't want to."

"What did you have in mind?"

"Something better." Eyes glinting, he leaned forward. "I don't know…maybe something that involves that pool."

"You want to go swimming?"

He shrugged. "Sure. Or at least go sit by there." Reaching out, he grabbed her hand and tugged her close. "I came over to see you, you know."

"Because?"

"Because I was missing you?" He brushed his lips over her brow. "And wanted to kiss you." He kissed her again, taking his time. She responded by pressing a little closer and meeting him halfway.

He tasted like iced tea and Tyler. Intoxicating. Their kisses slowed, became more thoughtful, thorough. Slowly she felt his hands run along her back, her hips. Down her thighs.

Remy shifted and ran her fingers through his hair. He sighed and plundered some more. Amazing how something so tame could last so long and could be so mesmerizing.

When Remy came up for air, she searched his face. "So, is that all you wanted to do?"

"No. But it will do for now. That and going for a swim."

"I was kind of thinking the same thing. Imagine that."

Warm heat lit his eyes. "Go put on a suit, Remy. We've got the whole evening."

As she turned and walked to her bedroom, Remy knew she couldn't be happier. After all this time, after all the doubts, she was finally happy again.

She hoped it would never end.

Chapter Nineteen

Tyler met her for a late breakfast at a popular beachside café the next morning. After filling him in on Carmen's sweet phone call filled with thanks, Remy said, "Thanks again for coming over last night. It was so thoughtful."

"Like I said, I was glad to help." Tyler was also glad Remy had called to ask for help with Marisol. He was happy he could offer some advice that she'd accepted. But that wasn't why he'd come over the moment Remy had called.

Fact was, he was willing to do whatever it took to be near Remy. To help her. To make her smile and look at him in that loving way that made his heart slam into his chest.

He would have come over to help change light bulbs, if that was what she'd needed.

As she sat across from him, the hem of her sundress fluttering lightly in the wind, Tyler scooted close enough in his chair to touch his knees to hers. "So, what's on your agenda for the rest of the day?"

"Nothing."

"Really?"

Looking at him curiously, she said, "Why are you acting like that's a surprise?"

"Because I've rarely seen you without plans."

A slow smile lit her face. "Then look again, because I called off of work. I've got the whole afternoon and evening open." She paused. "What about you?"

"I was thinking about going to play some golf down at Emerald Isle. Do you play?"

"Not really. But I drive a mean golf cart. Care for a lady chauffeur today?"

"I can't think of a better offer I've ever had."

TYLER HADN'T LAUGHED so much in ages. Remy was as capable at driving a golf cart as she was at doing just about anything else. But what struck him as funny was her lack of concern for the game.

Oh, she sat patiently when he teed off. She walked by his side along the greens. But, her mind definitely wasn't on the game.

No, she looked in creek beds for fish and turtles. She pointed out squirrels and birds. She teased him about how he couldn't putt to save his soul—and for once, he took the criticism with a grin instead of using it as an excuse to be more competitive.

In between his tee shots and waiting for the foursome in front of them to find their golf balls, they talked. He learned about her childhood, growing up in a Midwestern town and playing "ghosts in the graveyard" and "capture the flag" with the other neighborhood kids.

In return, he told Remy about his parents and their love for each other. And about how he couldn't abide spinach.

She mentioned that she happened to love vanilla ice cream and ripe peaches in the summer. And how she'd never been able to say no to a new shade of lipstick.

He told her he liked kissing her lips, no matter what shade they were.

By the time Remy guided the car off the path and into the parking lot adjacent to the pro shop, Tyler felt as if he'd known her forever.

HAD THINGS BEEN SO EASY with Mark? Remy couldn't remember. They'd dated for years, and had the type of easy relationship that had stood up to a great many obstacles. Underneath all that romantic love was a deep, all-encompassing respect for each other. And friendship. With Tyler, everything was happening in a rush. So fast, she didn't want to be without him. It was almost as if she couldn't bear to even look away from him. And that's when Remy knew she'd fallen in love. Knew she was finally ready for anything in their relationship.

She'd enjoyed watching him traipse across the course, so confident and sure of himself in his bright white golf shirt. She liked how he made each shot with precision, but didn't really seem to care what his score was.

She liked his compliments and the way he always seemed to make her feel like the prettiest girl in the room.

After placing his clubs in his trunk, he said, "You up for some dinner? There's a place near my condo that has great fish tacos."

"I'd love to go there. If you let me see your place."

"It's nothing fancy," he warned. "It's just a two-bedroom condo."

"I don't need fancy."

Twenty minutes later they arrived at his condo. She couldn't help but tease him as she looked around. "This sure is some shack. It's gorgeous."

"Oh, well, I've been redecorating a little bit."

"A little?" She pointed to the pewter clock and the antique surfboard hanging over the fireplace. At the arrangement of black-and-white photos of the area, each encased in silver frames and mounted against a background of butterscotch wall. "You just threw this all together?"

He shrugged good-naturedly. "Well, actually, I did have some help. Cindy has a neighbor who's an interior designer. She brought over a couple of things to see if I'd like them. I did."

Remy couldn't help but run her hand along the copper-colored leather couch. "I do, too."

"I'm glad. Actually, I do have a secret. I was hoping one day you would come over. And if you did, I didn't want there to be anything that you might find fault with."

"Because?"

"Just because. How about we keep it at that?" After showing her the guest bedroom, laundry room and back screen porch, he shrugged. "Are you ready to walk down to the taco place?"

"Almost. You haven't shown me your bedroom."

When he hesitated, she tugged on his hand. "I know what I'm asking, Tyler," she murmured.

"You sure?"

"Positive."

"All right, then." When he linked his fingers through hers and tugged, she followed him gladly. Finally she was at peace with both her past and the present, and more than eager to share her body with him.

However, all thoughts of romance were pushed to one side when he pushed open a pair of white French doors. "Oh, my."

"Meredith said this was her crowning achievement."

"I can see why. Tyler, this is beautiful. I've never seen

a room done in shades of brown and light blue before."
She pointed to the bay window, dressed in luxurious
panels of nubby silk that gathered at the floor, to the
dark brown rattan chair next to a reading table. At the
charcoal etchings of sailboats. "It looks like something
out of a magazine."

"Like I said, I had some help." When she looked
around the room again, he stepped in front of her so she
couldn't see anything but him. "You know, I brought you
here with the most innocent of reasons."

"But now?"

"Now that you're sure…" His gaze turned sheepish.
"How about we admire the room another day?"

She blinked, daring to tease. "What room?" She
rested her palms on his chest. "All I see is you."

"Good answer." Strong arms circling her, he smiled.
And then, before she could comment on that, he lowered
his head and kissed her. Once again everything else
faded away.

Remy couldn't help but shudder in anticipation as
their lips met, then explored and meshed. Oh, but she
loved feeling his arms around her. Tyler had the best
shoulders—his muscles were so defined and perfect. His
chest was firm and smooth and solid. As she rose on her
tiptoes and pressed a little closer, his hands grasped her
hips. She buried her face in his shoulder as his tongue
traced a line down her throat.

Time blurred as desire intensified. She moaned as
their kisses slowed and hands roamed. Remy found herself eager to match each of his movements with a brush
of her lips and bolder caresses.

Oh, Tyler felt so good, and everything about him was
perfect. In no time at all she'd pulled his knit golf shirt

over his head and run her hands along his pectorals, enjoying how his muscles responded to her touch.

"Your turn," he murmured, sliding down the straps of her sundress. The wisp of her bra went next. With a shake of her hips, the rest of her dress slipped to the floor. Soon his shorts lay on the carpet, too.

And her panties.

As his gaze skimmed her body, Remy had never felt more beautiful. Everything in his gaze showed her his approval. Skin met bare skin as they embraced again, feeling so delicious. Feeling so empowering.

Moments later Tyler paused for a breath. "Bed."

She chuckled as he tossed back the comforter and sheets and tugged her forward. Smiling, Remy joined him on the cool cotton. As he moved to partially cover her body with his, she felt herself shiver. And then there was little time to think as they began to explore again. Touching, getting reacquainted. Touching and testing.

Just as things were about to spiral out of control, Tyler groaned. "Sorry. I almost forgot," he said sheepishly as he pulled open his bedside table's drawer and took out a square packet.

She blinked in surprise. After she and Mark had found out she couldn't bear children, she'd pretty much forgotten about the need for birth control.

As she saw him rip open the square and sheath himself, she almost told him there was no need. But then she reminded herself it would be best to be careful. Tyler had obviously led a full life before she came along.

Through the curtains, tiny lights began to sprinkle the horizon as the evening lights flickered on. In Tyler's room Remy fought for control as their kisses built in intensity, as featherlight touches turned demanding.

And then, with one thrust, he was inside her and

she wrapped her legs around his hips. But Remy was scarcely aware of anything except how dark his eyes looked as they stared into hers.

How wonderful his lips were when they smiled.

And how incredibly perfect the moment was between them. So real. So special.

This was right. She was in love. Everything was perfect, and she hoped this wonderful, wonderful feeling would go on forever.

Chapter Twenty

"So, one day, how many kids do you want to have?"
Tyler asked lazily around midnight. Right after they'd
taken a slow, hot shower together and found their way
back to his bed.

"Children?" In an instant her body stiffened. When
he raised an eyebrow in question, she fought for control,
forced herself to relax. "Oh, I don't know."

"Remy? You're all tense. Come here, baby. What you
need is a back rub."

What she needed was to be talking about anything
but kids. But she kept silent as he moved to the side,
guiding her to lie on her stomach.

After rubbing his hands together to warm them up,
he gently began to knead her shoulders, stopping for a
moment to carefully push her mass of hair to one side.
"Feel good?"

She couldn't lie. "Feels great. Ooh, don't stop."

Tyler gave her a little pat. "I'll rub your back as long
as you want me to."

Her eyes drifted closed as he massaged the skin along
her spine, stopping every so often to press his lips to
places his fingers had just vacated. Her body began to
buzz again as his hands drifted lower.

Perhaps they'd just make love again. They didn't need to talk....

But Tyler obviously didn't feel the same way. "Come on," he murmured just as he shifted closer, leaning down to playfully nip her earlobe. "Everyone thinks about babies. Have you ever thought about what you'll look like, all beautiful and pregnant?" He chuckled as he circled his arms around her rib cage and found her breasts.

As his fingers located her nipples, as her body responded to his touch, her mind froze. "No..."

He nipped gently on the back of her neck. "Would you be mad if I said I have? You're going to be gorgeous. I won't be able to keep my hands off you."

He paused, then kissed the back of her neck some more, just as his hands drifted lower. To her belly. "All right, honey," he murmured. "We don't have to talk about babies. Not yet."

The idea that she would never be able to be pregnant, that she'd never be able to give him what he wanted, made her run cold. With a jerk, she pulled away from the protective warmth of his arms. "I...I don't want to talk about babies."

"What?" He smiled. "Am I making you nervous? Don't be, Remy. I've got a whole box of protection. And...I know we don't need to be in a hurry." He shrugged. "I'm just looking forward to the day you're pregnant." His eyes darkened. "To the day we bring home a little sweetheart who looks just like you."

She swallowed. That was a nice fantasy.

But as she stared at him, as she saw the longing in his eyes, she couldn't bear to tell him the truth. Couldn't bear to say that what he wanted was never going to happen.

It made her too ashamed.

So she hardened her voice. "If you want to know the truth, I never think about having any kids."

He stilled. "What? You're kidding, right?"

"No, I'm not."

Hurt and something harder filled his eyes. "Why not? Is it because of your work? You're the boss. I'm sure they'll give you time off. And we could make things work out. All working mothers do these days."

"No, it's not that." She sat up a little more and pulled the sheet over her breasts, needing some kind of defense against his questioning gaze. "It's…it's because I don't think I'll ever have any."

Something fell from his expression. "Why?"

She heard the accusation in his tone and felt lower than ever. She hated admitting her faults. Hated that she had no control over her infertility.

Hated that Tyler was looking at her in the way he was. But because she loved him—wow, what a time to realize that—she decided he deserved the truth. The terrible, awful truth. "I had a pretty severe case of endometriosis in my twenties. I can't have children."

Though pride forced her to keep her head high—her physical problems were no fault of her own—inside, she wanted to hang her head in shame. No matter what the doctors said, not being able to bear children felt like an unbearable flaw.

But instead of giving her comfort, of saying that he understood, he fired another question. "Did you get a second opinion?"

"There was no second opinion to get. I was sick. My treatment was a trade-off—the result left me infertile. I knew it. Mark knew it. And, well, he understood."

A muscle jumped in his jaw at Mark's name. Remy

couldn't blame his reaction. She'd definitely thrown in her husband's name on purpose. Mark had been by her side when she'd first received the life-changing news. Mark had held her for hours while she'd cried.

Still staring at her in wonder, Tyler shook his head. "Remy, I had no idea you couldn't have children."

"It's okay. I like kids, but I've resigned myself to never having to make lunches for a crowd or to have to watch hours of cartoons." Inside, Remy winced. She'd intentionally made her words more superficial than she felt. But that was what she had to do.

Otherwise, even after all this time, she'd start crying.

Little by little she felt Tyler pull away, physically and emotionally. A minute later he slipped on boxers and a T-shirt and walked to the other side of the room. "I'm really surprised, Remy. I mean, I know you're forty-two, but it never occurred to me that you didn't have children because you couldn't have any. I thought it all had to do with Mark being sick."

Chilled, she pulled his comforter closer. "I...I know it's hard news to hear. But the good news is that other than that, I'm okay." She attempted to smile, but feared she merely looked sickly. "I just can't have any babies."

"But I really want children." With stiff movements he picked up his shorts and stepped into them. "I always have."

"I hadn't 'planned' on getting endometriosis, Tyler."

He ran a hand through his hair. "Maybe now things are different." With a gleam of hope, he said, "I'll call up Cindy's OB. She said he's great. I bet he'll know what you can do."

"No. There's nothing to do." She was hurt. He was acting as if she'd celebrated her physical state, when in fact, she'd done nothing of the sort. She'd only stated the facts…very reluctantly, too.

When he turned away, Remy slipped out of bed, hurriedly yanked on her underwear and fastened her bra. Then, feeling terribly exposed, she grabbed the rest of her clothes and strode to his bathroom. "I'll be out in a sec," she mumbled. "I just need a few moments to…" To what? Will herself not to burst into tears?

But even though she didn't finish the sentence, it didn't really matter—he obviously wasn't in the room any longer.

HE'D BEEN PACING the living room since he'd left the bed. Rarely before had he felt so conflicted. Usually he came to a decision, made it and then moved on.

That was the way to do things. That was the way to succeed. It had always worked before—in business and in his personal life. No sense making things more difficult than they had to be. No sense in prolonging problems.

But now it was different. He cared about her. From the moment he'd seen her photo and had read the biography, he'd known there was something special about her.

As they'd gotten to know each other, he'd become even more sure. With Remy, their differences didn't matter. He didn't care what she did, or if some people thought he was too young for her. All he'd cared about was the certainty in his heart that she was special. That they were special together.

And all those feelings had come about before they'd even slept together! And that…well, that had been great.

Now he was getting his just deserts, and that was a fact. Now he knew what it felt like to love someone but for it still not to be enough. It was hard and it was emotional, but he had only himself to blame.

He'd walked into their relationship with a whole perception about Ramona Greer in his head. Once more, even after discovering a number of new things about her, he still had never second-guessed his other assumptions. He should have asked more questions. He should have asked her what her personal goals were, how she saw herself living in two, five, ten years. Maybe he should have interviewed her the way she'd interviewed him.

But he hadn't. He'd just fallen in love with her while imagining she wanted the same things he did. He couldn't have been more wrong.

She didn't ever plan to be a mother. Didn't ever plan on building a swing set or sitting through soccer tryouts. She wasn't looking forward to barbecues and car trips and noisy dinners and homework sessions. Ever.

If he stayed with her, there'd never be Tonka trucks to trip over or *Sesame Street* blaring in the living room. No Barbies or stuffed teddy bears or sweet hugs or the sloppy baby kisses Megan and April greeted him with.

No Halloween costumes or cookies for Santa, either. No tooth fairies or Easter bunnies.

None of the dreams he'd clung to ever since his parents had died. None of the things he'd sworn he'd do because he hadn't done enough of them with his mom.

He couldn't say goodbye to it all. Not yet. Not at thirty-four.

When she made an appearance, he paused midstep, then forced himself to keep his expression neutral as he turned to face her. "Do you have your jacket?"

"Yes." Her bottom lip trembled. "I think you need to take me home. Now."

"All right, but first we should talk."

Looking stricken, she shook her head. "I'd rather not."

"It won't take long." When she laid her jacket on the back of a chair, he steeled himself to just tell her the truth. Waiting wouldn't make things easier. "Remy, there's no other way to say this.…"

"Then just say it."

"All right. I think we better break things off."

"Permanently?"

Although what he was doing hurt like hell, he forced himself to slowly nod. She blinked back a tear, causing another one to escape. His stomach knotted. Tyler forced himself to shift his gaze, to stare at the wall right to her left. She deserved his explanation, but it wasn't easy.

"You don't want to see me anymore…because I can't have kids?"

He felt horrible. But knowing how terrible he'd feel years from now…how much he'd grow to resent their childless state, how crushed he would be to never hold a child of his own, he hardened his heart. "Don't make it sound like this is easy for me. Listen, I care about you. I think I was falling in love with you, but I don't know if I can handle this. I came here to Destin to get married and start a family. It's important to me."

She winced. "I see."

"Do you? Remy, what we have now is terrific, but I want more. One day, I really want what Cindy and Keith have."

"And for that you need a woman who can have children."

He wanted a family one day. He wanted to be a father.

But he didn't bother clarifying. With Remy, it was a nonissue. "Yes." When the tears fell again, he felt so helpless, he felt so guilty, he lashed out. "I'm not trying to be unfeeling, Remy."

"But you just are." With an unsteady hand she swiped off another tear. "You are such a liar. I can't believe you said you were falling in love with me."

"I wasn't lying about that. I meant every word."

"No. If you loved me—if you really loved me—a future without a baby wouldn't matter."

"It does matter. If you loved me, you'd understand that it matters more than anything else in the world."

"Then I guess we're done talking, because there's really nothing else to say." In two jerky moves she picked up her jacket and clutched it to her chest, as if it was a shield. Then she strode to his front door. "I really need to get out of here right now. If you can't take me home, I'll call a cab."

"Of course I'll take you home." After grabbing his wallet and keys from the kitchen counter, he followed her outside to his car. The moment he unlocked it, she slipped in and buckled up, never glancing in his direction.

They sat in silence during the whole thirty-five-minute drive from his place to hers. The moment he stopped in front of her house, she opened her door and got out.

But he couldn't just let her walk away. Standing up, too, he turned to her. "Remy, I really am sorry."

"Is that right?" Instead of the crying woman he'd seen in his living room, a formidable lady turned to face him. "I don't know what kind of game you were playing, but I should congratulate you. You definitely won. You certainly played me well."

The comment stung. "I wasn't playing."

"From my perspective, it sure seems that way. You know, things happened between us because you pushed them, Tyler. *You pursued me.* I never would have sought you out. Never."

"Well, that's good to know."

Ignoring his retort, she continued. "I hope you'll remember that during all that pursuing and flirting and sweet looks…you never asked if I was worth your time. You never asked me questions about my uterus."

"Come on…"

She just kept talking. "Tyler, you made me think that you liked me for me. Even when I doubted us. Even when I fired you, you made me change my mind. You made me believe in us. You made me believe in love again." Little by little, her defenses crumbled before him. Her eyes turned watery and her bottom lip quivered. "I don't know if I can forgive you for that."

"I'm sorry you feel that way." He could have tried to explain himself some more, but there was no point. Besides, he felt horrible. Intellectually, he knew he could give up his dreams for a family, of being a dad, but in his heart he knew he just couldn't. Not yet. It was too important to him.

"I know you're sorry. But one thing is certain, Tyler. I promise you're not half as sorry as I am. Not half."

That, he knew, was wrong. He was extremely sorry. Sorry he'd tried so hard. Sorry he'd been so optimistic.

Sorry she didn't understand.

For the first time in his adult life he drove off before making sure his date was safely inside her house. He drove off, punched the accelerator and let the car fly.

Chapter Twenty-One

When Carmen arrived at Remy's on Monday morning, she was surprised to find Remy there. When she saw Remy's tearstained face, all notions of working flew out the window.

She fixed Remy a cup of hot herbal tea, planted them both on the couch and encouraged her to talk.

And talk Remy did. She told Carmen all about the golf game, how they'd gone to bed together…and then his horrible, terrible announcement.

"I'm sure he didn't mean those things he said," Carmen said soothingly. "Men don't have the words for all their feelings."

"I'm pretty sure Tyler does. He couldn't have been any clearer when he described his feelings," Remy replied. Feeling yet another torrent of tears approaching, she blinked rapidly. "I'm trying to be strong, but I'm just devastated."

Carmen handed her another tissue. "I know, but I feel sure everything will work out again in no time."

"I don't think so. He wants babies and car seats and strollers." Remy's head spun as she tried to recall Tyler's actual words, but that was the gist of it.

Of course, it was impossible to remember it all. He simply had wanted so much. So many things it wasn't possible for her to give. Sniffing loudly, Remy fought for control, but it was no use. She felt as if her heart had been stomped on and kicked to the curb. "Carmen, he wants all kinds of things I can't give him. I've never felt more inadequate in my life."

Enfolding her in a hug, the older woman patted her shoulder. "I'm so sorry, dear. I thought he was a good man, too."

From the moment he dropped her off, she'd been inconsolable, which was almost as hard to deal with as Tyler's words had been.

She'd known she was falling in love with him, but she hadn't imagined that he'd already claimed her heart. With a sniff, she muttered, "I guess Tyler still is a good man. I just wish things hadn't ended like they did."

"Is there nothing you can do?"

"Besides trying to get a fully functioning uterus? No. It's over."

"I see." After staring at Remy a moment longer, Carmen stood up and clapped her hands lightly. "I think we need sustenance, don't you?"

Like a pet, Remy followed Carmen into the kitchen, then pulled out the container of flour while Carmen got out eggs, butter and vanilla. In the first few weeks after Mark's death, when each day had meant hours sorting through hospital and insurance statements, writing thank-you notes for flowers and condolence gifts, Carmen had started baking with Remy.

Remy had enjoyed their camaraderie in the kitchen, and the simple joy of eating hot cookies fresh from the oven. "What are we making today?"

"I think peanut butter bars," Carmen announced after a peek into the pantry. As the butter and sugar blended under the electric mixer, Carmen said, "I hate to admit it, but I'm very sad. I liked Tyler, too. He helped Marisol so much." While pulling out the measuring cups, she paused, "Oh, my…do you think he'll forget about her now? Marisol has an interview on Friday. He promised he'd visit with her about it."

"I'm sure Tyler will continue to help Marisol." As she handed Carmen a measuring spoon and the box of baking soda, she added, "He's the same guy. He'll still do great things, I'm sure. He'll just do them without me."

Over the next fifteen minutes they worked side by side just the way they used to. The familiar routine felt as comforting as a warm hug, but the activity was also bittersweet.

Remy had thought she'd never need support like this again.

But she was also determined to stand on her own two feet very soon. "Tomorrow I'll go back to work and pretend this whole episode didn't happen."

"Maybe. Though if I were you, I'd remember what *did* happen. This Tyler got you going out. Soon, I bet you'll go out on another date once again. Now that you're ready." After measuring out the peanut butter, Carmen plopped it into the bowl with a satisfied nod, then turned the electric mixer back on.

"I don't know if I'm ready, per se."

"Oh, Señora Greer. You're ready. You should go find another man as soon as you can."

Remy chuckled. "Because they're all going to appear out of the woodwork?"

"Because they'll have heard that you're available. That's the secret." With a little grunt she pulled out a baking dish and slowly scooped the mixture into it, taking care to scrape the sides with a spatula. "Remember, I'm the one who watches *Oprah*. You should listen to my wisdom. I know."

"And in the meantime?"

Carmen smiled. "In the meantime we will eat peanut butter bars and have some more tea."

Holding up her cup, Remy saluted Carmen. "You are the wisest woman I know."

With a wink, Carmen smiled. "Tell that to my Marisol. If she ever learned to listen to me, it would save her a lot of trouble."

THE NEXT DAY AT WORK, things were so busy Remy didn't have a moment to sit until Shawn presented her with a neatly typed list at three o'clock. "What's this?"

"Your interviews. Remember when you said you wanted to be included in the process? Your first appointment will start in fifteen minutes."

Flipping through the folders, she glanced Shawn's way. "Anyone you think will be a good fit?"

"Maybe. It's hard to know before you meet them."

Summoning up a businesslike demeanor, Remy pulled out her glasses and a pen. "Thanks for getting all this organized, Shawn. Let me know when our first candidate arrives."

"Sure, Ramona." She looked at her sideways. "Um, are you okay?"

"Of course. Why?"

"Oh, I don't know. You just seem preoccupied."

Pretending to yawn, Remy stretched one arm out in front of her. "I think I'm just sleepy. I've, uh, had a couple of late nights lately. I'm fine."

Twenty minutes later Remy knew she was so very much not fine. Jacob Barnes had been sitting there across from her for ten minutes, telling her everything about himself. He had dark hair and dark eyes and was so like—and yet unlike—Tyler Mann that she wanted to cry.

"So that's why I decided to apply, Ms. Greer," he finished, resting his elbows on his knees.

She forced herself to concentrate on his qualifications. Not the way he was quietly looking her over. "Your hours are flexible?" she asked, though she didn't really care. Jacob would do fine at Carnegie no matter what shift they placed him in.

"Definitely." He flashed a smile. "I'm not married."

"Ah. When can you start?"

"Anytime. I'm ready."

Was there something vaguely suggestive in his responses? Or was she just reading something into his words? Either way, it slightly creeped her out.

Holding out a hand, she said, "Either I or Shawn, my assistant, will be contacting you."

He squeezed her hand. "I'll look forward to it."

Hastily she pulled her palm from his grip. Eager to put some distance between them, she opened her door and waved him out. "Good afternoon, Mr. Barnes."

He had the nerve to wink before he sauntered out of Shawn's waiting area and down the stairs.

As she watched him leave, she wrote a big *X* on his cover sheet. No way was she ever hiring a single man again.

Especially not one who looked to be on the prowl.

Or who had dark hair and dark eyes. Hmm. Maybe she should try to never hire another man.

She was just about to crumble Jacob Barnes's résumé and toss it in the trash when Shawn appeared, a smile plastered on her face. "Ms. Greer, this is Melody Evans. Your next interview."

"Pleased to meet you, Ms. Greer," Melody said as she held out a hand. "I sure appreciate you taking the time to meet with me today."

Melody was attractive, African-American and middle-aged. She was about as opposite from Tyler Mann as a person could get. Put that way, she was perfect. Shaking Melody's hand, Remy greeted her warmly. "I'm very happy to meet you, too, Melody. Let's go in and talk about Carnegie. We'll see if you're a good fit for our call center."

MELODY *had* BEEN a perfect fit. After checking two of her references, Remy had called Melody herself with the good news before five o'clock. She'd let Shawn deal with everyone else. They'd hired another woman, too, and a retired gentleman who'd once owned a hardware store. Jacob and a guy named Bob had been politely rejected.

Though Shawn had looked as if she wanted to question Remy's decisions, to her credit, she said nothing. At six o'clock Remy told her goodbye.

Now she was alone in her office. Downstairs, yet another shift of call operators was on duty. Remy supposed she could walk the aisles and see how everyone was doing.

There was a stack of mail that needed to be sorted through and the weekly report that needed to be finished and sent to Corporate.

Her parents' anniversary was coming up. She should fill out their card and make sure it got in the mail. She should order their flowers, too.

Yes, there were a dozen things she could be doing—if she wanted to do anything.

She did not.

Carefully she opened her refrigerator, pulled out a bottle of Perrier and sipped. Then she remembered chugging the drink as soon as Tyler left her office.

The memory inspired a torrent of tears. And because no one was there to see her do it, she sat back at her desk, turned toward the wall and cried.

Chapter Twenty-Two

"You've got to move on, man," Keith said three weeks after Tyler and Remy had broken things off. "Remember your goal? How you want a future, with a wife and kids? You can only get those things if you keep focused. Stay on target."

"It's not that easy."

"It's easy enough. Remy wasn't right for you." Keith punctuated his remark by opening another ice-cold bottle of beer. With little fanfare he handed another bottle to Tyler. "She doesn't have your goals."

Memories of their last conversation still stung. He'd felt as if he'd been sucker punched when she'd told him—so matter-of-factly—that she had no intention of ever having children. And when she'd simply shrugged when he'd asked what he was supposed to do with his dreams of having a family, of celebrating holidays with Cindy and Keith and April and Megan by bringing over a whole crew of his own.

Thinking of a future without all that, he couldn't do it.

But still…he'd thought she was in love with him. He'd thought she could've at least seen his point of view. But she hadn't even been willing to listen.

"I don't know what I'm going to do."

Keith grunted, as if Tyler was making a mountain out of a molehill. "Sure you do. You'll date again."

Twisting open the cap, Tyler took a fortifying sip, though he felt no enjoyment from the buzz that was overtaking him. Yeah, they were sitting on the end of the dock as they always did, and he enjoyed his brother-in-law's companionship the same as always, but he felt as if something inside of him had just died.

Keith sent a frown his way. "You look like death warmed over."

"I know. I just can't believe she didn't ever tell me that she couldn't have kids." Frowning, he remembered the moment he'd first pulled out that condom. She'd never said a word about how they had no need for birth control. Why hadn't she said something then? It would have made everything a whole hell of a lot easier.

Yeah, right, his conscience fired back. *Like you'd have run right out of that room.*

No, he would still have made love to her. He'd been dying for her. And dammit, it had been good, too.

Keith took a swig of his beer. "Of course, in Remy's defense, I imagine infertility is nothing a woman would be eager to talk about."

Sipping slowly, Tyler knew Keith's words had merit. "I imagine it would be really hard. Actually, Remy looked really broken up about the whole situation. Maybe a better man would have been able to brush aside his dreams and grab hold of new ones. But I'm just not ready to do that, Keith. Imagining being a father got me through a lot of dark days since my parents died."

"The whole situation sucks."

"It sure does." In unison they each took a pull from their bottle and stared silently at the Gulf waters. Tyler felt lost.

After a few moments Keith cleared his throat. "But work is going all right, right?"

Tyler chuckled. "If you can call what I'm doing work. Right now I'm kind of a one-man recruiting agency. The doctor's office who hired Marisol gave me a finder's fee. They said I'd saved them from hiring a big recruiting office to find a qualified applicant."

"I hope you took that fee."

"Oh, I did. But get this—almost as soon as Marisol signed her employment contract, she sent four of her friends from college my way. I've been talking with them, coaching them, too. Two have interviews this week. Actually, one of the guys is in the middle of his second round of interviews."

What he didn't feel like sharing was that Marisol had been sending him messages from Carmen, who was evidently keeping everyone up-to-date on Remy.

She was back to working sixty and seventy hours a week. She wasn't sleeping and she'd lost weight, too.

It didn't help his conscience to know that none of that was technically his fault. He still felt terrible knowing that he was the cause of her pain.

"It doesn't surprise me that you're good at recruiting," Keith said. "You have a way of seeing people's pros and cons within moments and being able to determine their best course of action."

"It's fulfilling," Tyler said modestly. Inside, the true satisfaction he felt by making a difference in others' lives lessened the complete sense of failure he felt in the relationship department.

"You know what Cindy's dying to tell you, don't you?"

"I can't imagine," he said dryly.

Keith ignored the sarcasm. "She thinks you should ask that Kaitlyn out."

"Kaitlyn? The girl from Carnegie? Why's she so keen on her? Cindy's never met the girl."

"But you've mentioned her more than just once or twice. Cindy thinks that's a good sign. Call her up, Ty."

"Maybe in a few weeks."

"You're not getting any younger. Take her out, have some fun. Give things a try. You know, it doesn't have to be serious."

"It won't be."

"But if it is, you'll have it made."

Tyler didn't like how that sounded. Have it made? It sounded as if all he needed was a baby machine. No, he wanted a relationship. A real one. He wanted love.

But maybe that wasn't everything.

"Come on, Ty. Make a girl happy."

"We'll see if she's all that excited to hear from me."

"I'm not talking about Kaitlyn—I'm talking about Cindy! If you ask Kaitlyn out, I'm going to be a hero. And I could use a little hero worship around the house. All I seem to do is change diapers and take out the laundry."

"Far be it from me to condemn you to a lifetime of that." Standing, Tyler stretched. "I will call Kaitlyn. It wouldn't hurt to go out with her, I guess. But tomorrow. Things are a little fuzzy right now."

Keith stood up too, a little unsteady on his feet. "I'm feeling fuzzy, too. Maybe you should spend the night here?"

Since it wouldn't do to drive, Ty readily agreed. "I will. But no more discussion about my love life. I can't take any more."

Keith slapped him on the back. "We just want you to be happy."

"I'm happy," Tyler proclaimed as he picked up the metal bucket, gathered the empties and started up the long walk toward the house.

Keith grunted, but Tyler didn't mind, since they both knew he was lying.

TWO DAYS LATER he picked up the phone and called Kaitlyn's cell.

"Tyler Mann," she said as soon as he introduced himself. "Now, this is a real surprise. How are you?"

"I'm fine. And you?"

"I'm good. Did you find another job?"

"More or less. I'm doing some work on my own. Are you still at Carnegie?"

She sighed audibly. "Of course. Where else would I be? It's my lot in life to be so good at something so bor-or-ing."

Tyler tried not to notice that she pulled her last word out to three syllables. "Listen, I called to see if you were free for dinner on Friday night."

"For, like, a date?"

"Yeah. If you aren't busy, that is."

She made him wait a good long minute. "Actually, I happen to have plans on Friday night."

"Oh. I see." Surely that wasn't relief he was feeling?

"But I'm free on Saturday night," she added in a rush. "That is, if you are."

Though he was tempted to say he was busy, his promise to Cindy and Keith was fresh in his mind. "Saturday night is good. How about I pick you up at seven?"

"Seven is great." After giving him her address, she said, "I'm really glad you called, Tyler."

She sounded sweetly sincere. Eager. "I'm glad, too," he finished before hanging up.

He just hoped he sounded as sincere as she did.

"CINDY, DO YOU AND KEITH want to meet me for drinks again?

"On your date with Kaitlyn?"

"None other."

Instead of jumping at the opportunity, she wrinkled her nose. "How many times have you gone out?"

"This will be our first date."

She chuckled. "Thanks for the offer, but I think we'll skip this one. Kaitlyn probably won't appreciate your sister joining y'all right off the bat."

Tyler imagined she wouldn't, but at the moment he didn't really care. He was not looking forward to the evening at all. In fact, he'd been kind of hoping they'd be around so he could be sure conversation wouldn't stall. "I don't know what I'm going to talk to her about."

"You? My Texas Casanova? Talk to her about whatever you usually talk to your women about."

He couldn't remember any women before Remy.

But since he was truly attempting to move forward, he murmured, "Thanks a lot for the advice."

"Oh, don't worry." Her eyes softened as she patted his arm. "It will be fun. Call me tomorrow and give me all the gory details. Better yet, come over around two. Keith's out of town, and I was going to spend an hour or so at the baby pool."

"See you then."

THE DATE HAD GONE WELL. Kaitlyn had looked stunning in a white halter-top jersey knit dress and strappy yellow sandals. She hadn't talked about diets at the casual beach restaurant he'd taken her to. Instead, she'd seemed to enjoy every bite of her tacos, chips and salsa.

Later, when the air had turned cooler and he'd draped his sport coat over her shoulders, she'd kept him amused while they sipped cocktails, sharing stories about different roommates she'd had.

She'd been the one who'd suggested they go for a walk on the beach. And as he'd held her hand and the gentle surf lapped the sand to their left, she'd looked perfect.

He learned there were a lot of good things to like about Kaitlyn. She did, indeed, love her mother. She babysat her brother's kids once a month so he and his wife could go to the movies.

In addition, she loved to travel, just as he did. Currently she was planning a trip to the Cayman Islands to snorkel and scuba dive—she'd just gotten certified.

And in her future, of course she wanted children— she wanted a whole houseful of them! Eyes shining, she relayed how her sisters had teased her, saying she was probably going to get as big as a house when she was pregnant, since all she'd ever talked about was enjoying every week of her pregnancies.

Later, when he'd walked her to her front door, she'd kissed him sweetly, but hadn't invited him in. And when he said he'd call her soon, she hadn't even attempted to play hard to get. Instead she'd given him a look filled with promise and said she'd look forward to it.

In short, Kaitlyn was pretty damn near perfect.

So why didn't he care?

Why wasn't he falling hard?

Chapter Twenty-Three

Almost reluctantly Remy slowly sat down in the wooden chair next to Mark's bed. It was 3:00 a.m. After attempting to read for a good thirty minutes, she'd gotten up, slipped on her favorite comfy robe and entered the guest bedroom.

"Mark, I think we've got to stop meeting like this," she said as she pressed the button to open the drapes. As her joke crashed and burned in the empty room, she leaned her head back and sighed. "Yeah, I know. I never was the life of the party, was I?"

Tonight, instead of the usual myriad twinkling stars and lights sparkling on the horizon, only a thick shroud of darkness greeted her. The lack of light suited her mood. Lately nothing had seemed positive or right, her mood had been so black.

Remy, why are you in here?

"I don't know," she answered. "And that's part of the problem. I don't know why I'm in here. It makes me sad, Mark. I used to have to struggle not to sit in here with you for hours."

That was never a good thing. You were supposed to have moved on. Remember?

"Lately I've been finding out that moving on is even

harder than I'd imagined. You know that guy I told you about? The pup? Well, he turned out to be a jerk."

They can't all be like me, Rem.

"Only you could joke about dating, Mark. The truth is, I've been in a pretty blue mood. Almost as bad as when you passed away. I don't know what to do."

Looking out the window again, she listened for his words of advice. But now none came. It felt as if he'd left the room. For the first time, she didn't feel his presence the way she usually did.

Actually, she felt nothing. It felt as if she was sitting in an empty guest bedroom.

"Mark?" She tried again, though whether she was hoping to hear from him, or for herself to feel the connection to him, she didn't know. Feeling discouraged, she slumped back against the chair with a sigh. Great. Now she didn't even have Mark's spirit to chat with.

Of course, perhaps it was because lately, she hadn't been thinking about Mark—she'd been thinking about Tyler. The guy who was still very much alive, and doing great, if the office gossip was to be trusted.

It seemed Kaitlyn had had a very nice evening with Tyler Mann. They'd gotten along so well, they'd even talked about babies and families.

"I don't know what to do anymore," she mused aloud. Then, with some shock, she heard her own conscience speak for her. *Go try again. Go out and live. Do something for yourself.*

It's time. It felt so much like a command, she did just that. She got up and left the room. It was time to take risks again. Even if she got hurt.

"MEGAN, YOU'RE WEARING me out," Tyler said as he held on to the girl with one hand and her fresh ice cream

with the other. In front of their feet lay the remnants of
her first cone…a casualty of Megan trying to skip and
eat at the same time. "Try and hold on to the ice cream
this time, 'kay?"

Blue eyes shining full of trust, Megan nodded. "Okay,
Uncle Tyler."

Just as it always did, his heart filled with love for her.
"I'd kiss your cheek, but you're a mess."

Megan giggled as Cindy trotted back with a handful
of wet paper towels, April riding in the jogging stroller
in front of her.

Thrusting a handful his way, she groaned. "Oh, Tyler.
Your shorts look like Megan smeared a whole gallon of
ice cream on them."

"It's no big deal, Cindy." Stepping backward, he
plopped the towels on his thigh and started pressing.
Looking around, he frowned. He supposed he looked
like an idiot, covered in ice cream, wiping himself with
towels, tripping over a little yappy dog.…

"Sorry, ma'am," he said when somehow the leash
looped around an ankle. "I wasn't looking and I…" His
voice drifted off as he saw who was at the other end of
that line. "Remy."

She looked more embarrassed than he felt. "Hi. I'm
sorry for the mix-up. I just got her, and I'm afraid she's
not used to a leash yet." She rolled her eyes. "I'm not
used to a leash yet."

Bending, he petted the tiny Scottish terrier. The puppy's curly black fur felt silky under his fingers and the
pink tongue made him smile. "You got a puppy?"

"I did." When Megan hurried over, then hesitantly
stared at Remy before reaching down to the pet, Remy
crouched down and smiled at the girl. "It's okay, Megan.
She doesn't bite."

Her eyes widened. "You know me?"

"No, we don't know each other, but I've heard a lot about you. I...I was friends with your uncle."

Tyler smiled at Megan as she cooed over the pup and experimentally patted its head, then rubbed the soft curly fur on its backside.

"Eat your ice cream, Megan. It's about to drip all over the dog," Cindy admonished, then smiled hesitantly toward Remy. "Hi there, Remy. It's nice to see you again."

Remy stood up. "Yes. You, too." Her eyes darted to Tyler's. In that gaze he saw a wealth of hurt and wariness.

His gut constricted. He'd put that wariness there. He'd put it there because he'd been so certain that his plan was the right one. His goals needed to be accomplished or he would be a failure. Why? Why had he been so certain he was right?

All at the expense of Remy—whom he'd claimed to love? If he'd been alone, he would have hung his head in shame. His parents would be so disappointed.

Another moment passed. Finally Remy cleared her throat. Backing up, she murmured, "Well, I was just taking Samantha for a walk. It's nice." She swallowed, looked flustered. "I mean, it's nice to see you, Tyler. All of you."

Cindy stepped forward. "You, too. Your puppy is adorable. Thanks for letting us see her."

Cindy nudged him just as Remy turned away. "Wait a moment, Remy. You named the dog Samantha?"

"Yes. It's after that show *Bewitched*. That was my favorite show when I was a little girl. My dad was allergic to dogs, so we could never get one, but I always promised myself I'd name my dog Samantha."

"I didn't know you wanted a puppy." Ouch. As soon as he said the words, he wished he could take them back.

She shrugged, looking somewhat confused herself. "I'm sorry you thought that. I guess there's lots we never knew about each other."

"I mean, I never heard you mention wanting a dog."

"I kind of figured it wouldn't be fair to own a pet, since I work so much, but then I realized it was really quiet in the house. And I started thinking that maybe I didn't need to work as much as I did." Smiling at Megan, who'd crept up and was petting the puppy again, Remy said, "Yesterday, when I was driving home from work, I passed the pet store and saw the for-sale sign. Next thing I knew, I was turning the car around."

"And saw her?" Megan asked.

"Well, it was kind of like that," Remy said. "Actually, the sign was advertising their rescue dogs. I thought a grown dog would be good. I'd give him a home and he'd give me some company. But then I saw Sam." She shook her head. "She was in this litter of six puppies, all squirmy and cute. I couldn't resist. When the volunteer plopped her in my lap, she nipped at my finger and gave this adorable little bark. It was just about the cutest thing I ever saw. After that, it was just a matter of filling out paperwork."

Watching little Samantha bark and yip and plop down on the grass, Remy looked at her fondly. "She's really cute, but a real mess."

"She's going to ruin that white carpet," Tyler pointed out.

Remy shrugged. "Oh, well. I never was too into all that white, anyway. I was getting tired of taking off my shoes all the time, if you want to know the truth."

Looking one more time at Megan and Cindy and April, she smiled a bit longingly, then put on a much more reserved smile for him. "Well, I guess I'll be on my way. Bye."

Not waiting for a reply, she turned and walked away, though it was slow going, since Samantha seemed determined to explore everything in their path.

As Tyler watched her walk away, he felt his lungs tighten. He was about to lose her.

He couldn't let that happen. He couldn't let Remy go. Not again. Not ever. Turning to Cindy quickly, he whispered, "I've got to go to her."

"I know."

"You understand?"

"She's who you love, Tyler. It's written all over your face." Staring at Remy's retreating form, she added, "And if I'm not mistaken, I think she just might be in love, too. Go."

"You think?" He was afraid to hope. Afraid to think everything between them hadn't been thrown away.

"I know...if you get a move on." She waved her hands in the air, shooing him away. "Go on now, Ty. I'll take the girls home and talk to you later. You get a ride with Remy. Or...call if things don't work out."

He hoped he wouldn't be calling his sister for a while. "Bye, girls," he said before turning and trotting after Remy.

Behind him, he heard Cindy laugh and Megan ask where Uncle Tyler was going.

For a moment he thought he'd lost Remy, but then he saw that she had turned a corner and was letting Samantha inspect a light post. "Rem, wait up."

She turned to him in surprise. "Tyler? What's wrong?"

"Not a thing." Now that he was standing in front of her, all the words jumbled in his head once again. "I was just wondering, could I walk with you?"

But instead of smiling gently, she remained guarded. "Actually...I don't think it's a good idea."

"I think it might be. Please, Rem? Can we walk together, just for a little while? I'd like to speak with you."

"What about Cindy and the girls?"

"They're going to go on. Besides, Cindy knows how important this is to me."

"I'm afraid I don't understand."

"If you let me walk with you for a while, you will. Please? I think there're things we need to talk about. After, if you don't want to see me again, I won't bother you anymore."

"Well, all right." Little Samantha plopped onto the ground, obviously exhausted. The sweetest expression came over Remy's face as she scooped up the little pup and cradled it in her arms. That look, that moment of tenderness wasn't something that could be faked.

With a sudden burst of clarity Tyler realized that had been the same look she'd given April when they'd run into each other buying movies. It wasn't that Remy didn't want children, or was afraid of children...it was that she wanted them so much and she was afraid of her longing.

That he could understand. He'd felt that way when his parents had died. He'd wanted a family so much but was so afraid it would never happen that he'd focused on work.

With the puppy securely in her arms, they started strolling down the beautiful walkways of the park. Around them, other couples walked, too. Every so often a jogger would zip by. But mostly it was couples of men and women, older ladies admiring the gardens, moms and their babies out for a stroll before nap time.

And them.

He glanced her way, but she said nothing, merely looked straight ahead. Obviously waiting on him.

Tyler turned over and over in his mind everything he'd thought he'd known about her. Finally, as they passed a lemonade stand and walked to a grove of orange trees, he said, "Look. I could tell you a thousand things, but at the heart of it all, at the core of everything, it all comes down to one thing. I've missed you."

To his shame, she visibly winced.

His heart sank. Well, it was no better than he deserved, Tyler supposed. Once again he was telling her his feelings and needs instead of focusing on her. "Let me try this again...."

"There's no need," she said sharply. "Things haven't changed, Ty. I still can't have children."

"That's okay."

"I don't think so. It was a pretty big deal a few weeks ago." Her voice was almost cool. Tyler realized she was trying her best to keep her emotions in check.

Not because she didn't feel anything. But because she felt too much.

How could he never have seen that? "I've been a fool, Remy. I thought things...I didn't give you enough credit or time...." Fumbling again, he said, "I hope one day you'll be able to forgive me."

"Maybe one day I will."

But not now. Slowly, carefully, afraid to find his way, he tried to explain himself. "When my parents died, I missed so many things. Things that I thought would never be obtainable. Because the thought of never having what my mom and dad had was so hard, I pushed it all to one side and concentrated on work. But work was a pretty poor replacement for love."

After checking to see that she was listening, he continued. "Then, after Cindy had such a difficult time with April, I moved here. But you know all that."

"Yes."

"Well, I made a plan. I wanted to get married and start a family right away, within a year. I'd gotten so used to obtaining my goals in business, I'd forgotten that people don't work that way."

"I've gotten caught up in work, too, Tyler."

"But unlike you, I was so blind. See, when you said you couldn't have any children, I panicked. I was afraid of putting away all my dreams. But now I realize that was wrong."

"What do you mean?"

"I mean, if you don't want to ever have children—not even adopting any—I'll learn to accept that."

Her eyes widened. "Tyler? Tyler, are you saying—"

"Please let me finish. See, Megan and April are awesome. I'll make do with being their uncle. That's fine. Because it doesn't matter what I don't have. What matters is that I'll have you."

"Did…did you really say you'd consider adoption?"

"Well, yeah. I mean of course I would."

A lump formed in his throat as her eyes filled with tears.

"M-Mark never would consider it."

He wasn't sure about the right thing to say. All he could add was what was in his heart. "Listen, I know your husband was a good guy," he said slowly. "A great guy. Maybe he had reasons for never wanting to adopt.

But I'm not him. I love kids. Any kids. I'd be thrilled to adopt, if that's what was in the cards."

Her legs looked unsteady as she turned away from him. He watched her put the puppy down and breathe deeply. "When we argued...we never talked about adoption."

"I know that. I wish we had." He'd been such a fool. Why hadn't he given her more time?

Two tears ran down her cheeks. "When you left, I was devastated. I thought you'd never want a woman who was flawed."

He couldn't help himself. With two fingers he gently swiped at her tears. "You're not flawed, Remy. You're perfect. I should have told you that."

"The truth is...I've always wanted children."

Reaching for her hand, he linked his fingers through hers, searching her beautiful face. "Please forgive me. Please forgive me for not talking this through with you." To his surprise, he was feeling a bit choked up himself. "I'm so sorry I just dropped you home and let you go."

"I'm sorry I let you." Next to her feet, the puppy woke up with a bark, then stretched and explored. Remy chuckled as the black ball of fluff raced after an old napkin, then abandoned it for a tiny twig.

Tyler watched her, watched the puppy and had never felt more at a loss of what to do or say. "Will you take me back?"

"I heard you were dating someone new."

"I was, but after the first date, I told her things couldn't work out. I only want you, Remy. So, will you?"

When she still stood motionless, he began to get desperate. "We don't have to pick up where we left off. How about we just take things slow? You know, meet for dinner?"

"Tyler, I just don't know if we were meant to be together."

"I know we were. I know it."

"I don't know…"

Directing her to a nearby bench, he said, "I've got something to tell you. Something about the real reason I came to Carnegie."

She scooted away so only their knees were touching. "And that was?"

"One day almost a year ago when I was flying on Carnegie Airlines, I was flipping through the in-flight magazine. Then all of a sudden I saw your photo."

"What?"

"Honest to God, that's what happened. I read about you in a magazine, I saw your photo and I knew I had to meet you."

Surprise and astonishment—and pure distrust— flickered in her eyes. "That's the craziest thing I've ever heard! No one does that."

"I did. And I know it doesn't make sense. But I don't think it has to." Impulsively he reached for her hand. "Don't you see, Remy? You've already got me. You've had me from the first time I saw your pretty gray eyes in a photograph." Running a thumb over her knuckles, he gazed at her. "Please, Remy. Please give me a chance. Give us another chance."

For a split second he thought she was going to nod. He thought bells would go off, fireworks would appear and everything was going to be super again.

But she only sighed. "What you told me, the magazine, the…the adoption…I need some time."

It took everything he had to simply nod. To let go of her hand. "Okay, then. You have my number."

For a moment she bit on her bottom lip, studying

him. Then she blurted, "Would you like to come over for dinner tomorrow night?"

"Yes."

"I thought I'd cook. Did you know I can cook?" she said in a rush. "I can. Pretty well, actually."

"I'll look forward to dinner. What time?"

"Seven?"

He stood up before she could take back the invitation. "I'll see you then. Thank you, Remy." When he turned and walked away, for a second he thought he heard her crying.

But he kept walking. Kept walking and holding that invitation close to his heart. She'd invited him over for dinner. They weren't over yet.

She wanted a family.

They had a future. He felt like pumping his fist in the air and shouting for joy.

He settled for walking the two miles back to his house and remembering every little thing she'd said.

Chapter Twenty-Four

Do not apologize. Do not make excuses. Imagine you're at work and in control.

Well, those three statements sounded fine, but as Remy looked in the mirror, she had a pretty good idea that not a bit of it was sinking in. In the mirror she looked unsure, nervous, eager to please and frumpy.

Tilting her head to one side, she considered changing again. Jeans and the white-on-white embroidered blouse were like nothing Tyler had ever seen her in.

Her hair in a loose ponytail was unusual, too. It looked plain and simple. Her flip-flops weren't very fashion-forward, either. Shoot, they weren't even fashion-backward.

No, she looked like Ramona Greer. Forty-two years old, and on some days, looking and feeling every day of it.

As Samantha tore around the corner, a pair of Remy's panty hose in tow, she knelt and started laughing. "What are you saying, pup? That it's time I gave these up—or that they're the perfect tug-of-war toys?"

Yip!

Grabbing one end, Remy tugged gently, bringing the little pup skittering forward with a tiny growl. Remy had just tugged a bit when the doorbell rang. "Here we go, Sam. Wish me luck."

Samantha yipped another bit of encouragement just as Remy opened the door to Tyler…dressed in pressed khakis, starched white dress shirt, red silk tie and blue blazer. Her eyes widened as he stepped inside. "Tyler. You look so nice. I guess I should have told you it would be casual."

His gaze had to be her mirror image. Dark eyes seemed to examine every inch of her faded jeans and shirt. "I've never seen you dressed like this," he said after what felt like forever.

Though she held her chin up, her toes curled inward. "I…I decided that it was time for you to see what I really look like. When I'm not trying so hard."

A slow smile curved his lips, though his eyes looked as serious as ever. "What were you hoping I'd see?"

"Someone who is over forty and can't turn back time."

"I don't want you to do that—I never have. I think you're gorgeous. I like every bit of your years." Raising his left hand, he handed her a rectangular box wrapped in silver paper. "I brought you something."

It felt heavy. "You didn't have to do that."

"I did. But if you don't mind…would you wait before you open it?"

"Okay." As Sam barked around Tyler's heels, Remy led the way into the kitchen. "I hope you like grilled steaks, potatoes and salad."

"I'm a guy. Of course I love steak."

She smiled. "Everything's ready but the steaks. I thought we could grill them while we sip some beer and talk?"

"Whatever you want, Remy. But if you don't mind, I'm going to take off the jacket and tie."

"I don't mind." She looked away so she wouldn't be standing there like a voyeur, watching him remove his clothes. To keep herself occupied, she pulled out two bottles of beer, set them on the counter, then grabbed the plate of steaks and headed out to the back patio.

Just yesterday she and Carmen had nailed up chicken wire on the railing. Now the puppy could roam free without Remy living in fear that she'd slip through the wide gaps.

Tyler noticed it the moment he stepped out. "You've been busy."

"I have. Carmen and I were pretty proud of ourselves, nailing all this up yesterday." Playfully she flexed her arm. "I'm stronger than I look."

He laughed. "I'll remember that." When he picked up the tongs for the grill, she noticed he'd slipped his loafers off and was walking around barefoot. He caught her look of surprise. "I'm trying hard to fit in today, I guess."

His self-deprecating way created a little buzz inside her. Things were different. Before, he'd always been so confident. So assured about what he wanted. She'd never had a moment's doubt that he wanted her—she'd just never been sure why.

Maybe that was why his rejection had hurt so much. It had felt as if the moment he'd realized she wasn't everything he wanted, he'd dumped her.

Now, though, he seemed far more quiet. Contemplative.

Oh, as he flipped steaks and she served dinner, they were as talkative as ever. She told him about the fire drill at Carnegie and the new round of people she'd interviewed. In turn, Tyler shared how Marisol was liking her new job and how happy that made him feel. He talked about how two of her friends had introduced him to a few more people, and an old buddy of his in the medical center had asked if Tyler could help him hire an office manager. "I can't believe how it's all taken off."

"Marisol thought you were wonderful. You really helped her."

"I'm good at managing people, and I really do like working for myself."

"I can see that."

Pushing his plate away, he murmured, "Remy, what I meant to say is that I'm pretty good at telling other people what to do. But as for myself? I need a lot of help. I've made some pretty big mistakes."

Remy wasn't eager to rehash everything again. Turning to the silver-wrapped box, she said, "When can I open it?"

"In a minute. I, um, wanted to tell you something first."

"Yes?"

"Remy, I love you. I love you and I adore you and I want to be with you the rest of my life."

She was stunned. Barely twenty-four hours ago she'd been sure she was going to be alone forever. That she'd never be good enough for him. Now he loved her. Forever? "What…what are you saying?"

"I'm saying that I hope that one day you'll love me, too. Enough to marry me."

"You're proposing? Right now?"

"Please don't be scared. We don't have to do anything right away. I just wanted you to know that before you opened the box."

"Well, now I'm really curious about what's inside."

Like a kid on her eighth birthday, she picked up the box and gave it an experimental shake. The contents shook a bit. "I love presents."

White teeth flashed. "I know you do."

For a moment she slid her hands over the slick paper, then tore back the wrapping. Inside was a shoe box. "What in the world? Did you buy me golf shoes?"

"No, I did not. Keep going, Remy." Though his words were confident, his voice lacked its usual self-assured tone. "You're about to get to the good part."

When she opened the lid, no shoes were inside…and nothing small and sparkling, either. No, there was only a file folder waiting. Holding it in her hands, she looked at him curiously. "What is this?"

A dimple appeared, making him look more like himself. "Take it out and see."

Slowly she lifted it open. There was a whole array of papers, some stapled together, others clipped. All looked very official. At the top of the stack lay a pink Post-it note. The following Tuesday's date was circled. Now she was completely confused. "What is all this?"

Looking unsure again, he cleared his throat. "They're papers. And the note is because we have an appointment scheduled for next week."

"With whom?"

Reaching out, he gripped her hand. "It's with the director of an international adoption agency." Her hand started shaking as he continued. "See, Cindy and Keith know a couple who adopted a baby from China three years ago. Cindy said they'd done a lot of research, so I decided to call them. They said this gal was the best. She specializes in couples who've never adopted before."

Remy was so stunned, she didn't think she could breathe.

His smile faltered. "See, I thought we could meet with her. If you, ah, wanted to. And, Remy, I'm not trying to make decisions for you, or force you to do anything you don't want to…but I thought together, we could just see.…"

Questions piled on top of one another, stuck on her tongue. *Breathe!* she coaxed herself. *Speak!* "You looked into adoption agencies? For us?"

A faint sheen of sweat appeared on his forehead. "Well, I called up the lady, who let me stop by her office and pick up all this. I was going to wait to schedule something until after we talked. But she had a cancellation, and her next available day after that was three months from now. She's, um, really busy." Looking at the paperwork in her hands, he added, "I don't want to force you to do anything you don't want…I don't want to push.…"

"I can't believe you did all this in one day's time. It's impressive."

"I don't know.…" Wearily he exhaled. "Please remember that we can cancel the appointment if you want. Please remember that no matter what, I love you, and I want to marry you."

"No matter what."

He nodded, looking miserable. "One day, if things work out, I want to go to China or Guatemala or Russia or wherever they have kids who want us and hold our child."

"Our child." She knew she sounded like a broken record. She knew she should say more than simply repeat his words, but her heart was beating so loudly, her emotions were so high, she could hardly process everything.

His expression turned bleak. "Hey, look, I'm sorry.

I don't know why I thought you'd be happy about this. I mean, here I go again, making plans...." He slowly stood up as his words faded. "Listen, I'll go."

"Stay."

He sat down again as Samantha yipped at his bare feet.

As Remy gazed at Tyler, the past few years spun in her mind. Spun and sorted themselves, and spit out memories. Learning that she could never become pregnant. Mourning for Mark. Working hours and hours of overtime.

Nights spent in an old wooden chair talking to thin air. Watching movies alone.

Meeting Tyler. Sailing with him. Their first kiss. The way his cheek dimpled when he was happy. Making love with him...and then feeling as if she was less than perfect.

And now.

As the silence continued, Remy struggled to find her voice. "The things you said...those papers, this meeting...it's the nicest thing anyone's ever done for me. Ever."

He blinked, then slowly smiled. "Yeah?"

She nodded. "You've given me back my dreams. I—I'd given up on falling in love again until I met you. I'd given up all the dreams I'd had of holding a baby, of going to ballet recitals, of little hugs and bedtime stories...." Her voice drifted off. "Tyler, thank you."

Moving closer, he pulled the box out of her hands. Set it on the table. Linked his fingers through hers. Pressed his palms against her own so that she felt his strength. Felt his warmth.

His confidence in her. In them.

"Remy, do you love me, too?"

"I've never stopped." She blinked away the rush of emotion.

He flashed a smile. "Remy, one day, will you marry me? I promise, you don't have to be alone. There're a million guys who would give a lot to be by your side… but I can also promise that no one will love you more. Will you marry me and be my wife?"

With Mark, the proposal had been straight out of a little girl's fantasy. Mark had presented her with pink sweetheart roses and a two-carat diamond ring and had gotten down on one knee.

When he'd proposed, she hadn't thought about cancer and sickness and loneliness and death.

But here was Tyler, asking her simply. No ring in his hand…only the most precious thing she could ever hope for—a future.

And there was only one answer to give. "Of course I will," she said softly. "Yes to you and marriage and adoption agencies and everything else. Because I love you, too."

With a yell, Tyler Mann wrapped his arms around her waist and spun her around. At his feet, little Samantha barked and yipped and danced on the patio.

In the distance, waves crashed in the Gulf, seagulls flew overhead and a thousand things that always happened—happened again.

While Ramona Greer—who went by Remy to all her friends—finally started living again.

Epilogue

"Are you tired, honey?" Tyler asked as he pulled off the freeway and started navigating the way back to their home.

Her head still resting against the car's headrest, she opened one eye. "I'm more tired than I thought was humanly possible."

Tyler reached for her hand. "Just think, in less than five minutes we'll be home."

"I can't wait." Remy curved both her hands around Tyler's. Unable to stop herself, she paused for a moment to admire the way their hands looked together. Tyler's hand was tanned and finely proportioned, long fingered and strong. Hers was slim and pale and so much smaller. Together, they looked so right.

Of course, a glance at her left hand wouldn't be complete without pausing to admire her ring. She never would have admitted it, but platinum suited her. So did the spray of diamonds that were embedded in the band.

She was unmistakably married—and unmistakably happy.

Looking her way again, Tyler murmured, "When we get home, I'll take care of things for a bit so you can nap."

"I'll be all right, though I may fight you for the shower."

He chuckled. "Remy, don't you know by now that I'll give you anything you want? You can have the shower first, no problem."

Oh, he spoiled her. He made her feel so loved and cherished. Remy hoped she'd never take his tenderness for granted.

Almost as much as she hoped she could maybe get just one hour of sleep sometime soon. She really was so, so tired.

When she opened her eyes again, it was to see Tyler pulling onto the circular driveway that framed her house—their house now. As he turned off the ignition, he met her smile with one of his own. "We made it."

"Why are we parking here?" They almost always parked in the garage.

"I'll move the car later, Remy. Don't fuss. I just thought it would be easier to unpack the car out here on the driveway. You know how cramped that garage is." With a smile, he opened another door in his four-door, very staid, brand-new BMW. "Besides, now we won't have to wait another moment to show Cassidy her room."

As Remy watched Tyler lift a very sleepy Cassidy into his arms, taking special care to support her head, she fought against tears.

Now they were a family.

A flurry of emotions rushed forth—happiness, wonder, the overpowering feeling of thanksgiving. They had so much to be grateful for. And so much to look forward to.

The past year had been a whirlwind. They'd married only two months after Tyler proposed, about the same time a chunk of their paperwork for the adoption agency was due. Remy had felt so proud and excited to write Ramona and Tyler Mann on all of the forms…and had been overwhelmed at the amazing amount of paperwork that was needed to adopt. Everything had had to be just so…certified and notarized and copied in triplicate.

Then they'd been fingerprinted and had attended workshops and answered hundreds of questions.

Next came a flurry of home visits and meetings with counselors and advisers. They'd waited and waited for everything to be processed.

Then came several months of close calls. Remy had been a roller coaster of emotion as she waited day after day for news. And then finally, at 7:00 p.m. on a rainy Thursday, the phone had rung.

A baby had been matched to them. Just for them. A few weeks later, Cassidy's photo had arrived in the mail. And just six weeks after that, they'd gotten the phone call they'd both been anxiously awaiting.

Cassidy's paperwork was complete. They were allowed to go to China to get her.

Of course, nothing was quite that easy. They'd had a few other dozen hiccups along the way. But she and Tyler had learned patience and had kept as positive as they could. They'd transformed the guest bedroom into the one that Remy had always been afraid to dream about…a perfect little girl's room.

They had packed their bags with formula and diapers and baby clothes and toys. A hundred things they were sure they'd need in China.

But then, just like childbirth must have been for other moms, all the stress and worry faded away the moment they saw their girl. Cassidy was five months old. She had beautiful silky black hair. Perfect ivory skin. And the sweetest, most angelic smile Remy had ever seen.

Now, after almost twenty-four hours in planes and airports, they were about to finally bring her home. It was almost overwhelming, she was so excited.

But maybe…maybe Tyler had had a different sort of homecoming in mind. "Are you upset we didn't let anyone come meet us at the airport, Ty?"

"Nope."

"Are you sure? I mean, at first I wanted this time just for us, but if you want, we could call some people. You know, see if they're free. Actually, it might be nice to show Cassidy off…."

Tyler only smiled as he passed their sleeping bundle into her arms. "Here you go, Mommy. I want to watch you bring our daughter inside for the very first time."

She didn't know if she'd ever lose the lump in her throat. "Thanks."

When he walked by her side, she glanced at the car, packed to the gills. "What about all our stuff?"

"Don't worry. I'll bring it in in a little bit."

"Oh. All right." As he fished in his pocket for the house key, Remy's mind started spinning. "Gosh, I just wish I'd had time to finish those curtains I was making."

"Cassidy won't notice."

"And diapers! I don't think we'll have enough for more than four days."

He laughed. "If Cassidy goes through two packs of Pampers tonight, I'll run to the store. I promise. Now, stop fussing," Tyler said as he unlocked the door and held it open for her. For them.

Remy stepped inside. As the cool air fanned her cheeks, little Cassidy popped open her eyes.

"This is home, Cass," she told the little angel who was looking around the entrance with a wide-eyed expression. "You're going to be so happy here."

Behind her, the door clicked. Wrapping an arm around her shoulders, Tyler said, "Let's go show the baby the kitchen."

"What?" Now he was really making no sense. "Ty, don't you think—"

"Hush. And don't forget to smile."

Before she could even wrap her mind around that comment, Tyler called out, "We're home!"

"Surprise!"

From out of the kitchen poured what had to be at least fifty people, all smiling and clapping and cheering.

Stunned, Remy looked from one beaming, crying, happy face to the next. There were her parents, all the way from Kansas City. There was her brother, Tim, with his wife and their four kids. Right out in front were Carmen and Miguel and Marisol and a few other members of the Rodriguez family. Shawn and Eddie were there, too. And so were Cindy and Keith and Megan and April.

And even more special, there were Mark's parents, crying unashamedly, showing her how much they loved her...how happy they were for her. And...how it was okay for her to continue living.

Turning to Tyler, Remy murmured, "Did you know about this?"

His smile looked to be a mile long. "Yep." Kissing the top of her head, he added, "I planned it all."

"How? How were you able to get hold—"

He stopped her words with a little tug forward. "We'll talk later. For now, go show off our baby, honey. Everyone's waiting."

Remy looked down at Cassidy, who miraculously hadn't started crying from all the commotion. She looked at Tyler, who had given her a future when she'd thought her life was over.

And then she looked at all their family and friends and knew she was so lucky and blessed. Finally she spoke. "Come meet Cassidy. Come meet our little girl."

When a little round of clapping and cheers rang out, Remy knew she had everything in the world she'd ever wanted...everything she'd ever dreamed of.

"Thank you, Tyler," she murmured when he wrapped his arm around her shoulders. "Thank you for taking a chance on a photo in a magazine."

His dimple appeared. "You're very welcome. Of course, the pleasure was all mine," he added just as everyone rushed forward and pulled them into a hug.

* * * * *

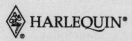
HARLEQUIN®

American ★ Romance®

COMING NEXT MONTH

Available July 13, 2010

#1313 THE LAWMAN'S LITTLE SURPRISE
Babies & Bachelors USA
Roxann Delaney

#1314 DEXTER: HONORABLE COWBOY
The Codys: The First Family of Rodeo
Marin Thomas

#1315 A MOM FOR CALLIE
Laura Bradford

#1316 FIREFIGHTER DADDY
Fatherhood
Lee McKenzie

HARCNM0610

HARLEQUIN®

A Romance

FOR EVERY MOOD™

Spotlight on

— Heart & Home —

Heartwarming romances
where love can happen
right when you least expect it.

See the next page to enjoy a sneak peek
from Silhouette Special Edition®,
a Heart and Home series.

CATHHSSE10

*Introducing McFARLANE'S PERFECT BRIDE
by USA TODAY bestselling author Christine Rimmer,
from Silhouette Special Edition®.*

Entranced. Captivated. Enchanted.

Connor sat across the table from Tori Jones and
couldn't help thinking that those words exactly described
what effect the small-town schoolteacher had on him.
He might as well stop trying to tell himself he wasn't
interested. He was powerfully drawn to her.

Clearly, he should have dated more when he was
younger.

There had been a couple of other women since Jennifer
had walked out on him. But he had never been entranced.
Or captivated. Or enchanted.

Until now.

He wanted her—*her,* Tori Jones, in particular. Not just
someone suitably attractive and well-bred, as Jennifer had
been. Not just someone sophisticated, sexually exciting
and discreet, which pretty much described the two women
he'd dated after his marriage crashed and burned.

It came to him that he…he *liked* this woman. And that
was new to him. He liked her quick wit, her wisdom and
her big heart. He liked the passion in her voice when she
talked about things she believed in.

He liked *her.* And suddenly it mattered all out of
proportion that she might like him, too.

Was he losing it? He couldn't help but wonder. Was
he cracking under the strain—of the soured economy, the
McFarlane House setbacks, his divorce, the scary changes
in his son? Of the changes he'd decided he needed to make
in his life and himself?

Strangely, right then, on his first date with Tori Jones, he didn't care if he just might be going over the edge. He was having a great time—having *fun*, of all things—and he didn't want it to end.

Is Connor finally able to admit his feelings to Tori, and are they reciprocated?
Find out in McFARLANE'S PERFECT BRIDE
by USA TODAY bestselling author Christine Rimmer.
Available July 2010,
only from Silhouette Special Edition®.